The Squeaky Ghost Gets the Curse

A HEX ON ME MYSTERY
BOOK THREE

KENNEDY LAYNE

THE SQUEAKY GHOST GETS THE CURSE

DEDICATION

Jeffrey—To my partner in all things to do with haunted houses!

Cole—Not sure about a haunted forest, but we can definitely give it a try one day!

Things go bump in the night in this hauntingly riveting tale in the Hex on Me Mysteries by USA Today Bestselling Author Kennedy Layne...

Lou can't even manage to dip a chocolate chip cookie into her glass of cold milk without getting a premonition of murder. Her unsettling vision is different this time around, though. The victim was practically thrown down a spiral staircase by...an invisible force right out of thin air!

Lou has no doubt that a murder was committed, and now it's a race against time to determine why. Unfortunately, Lou and the gang know they'll be too late to stop an affluent widow from meeting her fate. All they can do is figure out who killed the reclusive woman in order to give her grown children some sort of closure while saving them from a similar fate.

All is not what it seems, though. As things begin to go bump in the night and strange noises eerily echo throughout the ancient mansion, Lou is left wondering if the culprit isn't a vengeful spirit with a purpose. You might want to keep the lights on for this scary ghost story—it promises to be a jumping cool time!

Chapter One

THE CRACKLES AND pops of the logs inside the small circle of stones caused glowing embers to rise up into the night sky along the near vertical path of the rising smoke. The smoldering swirl was hampered only by the mere hint of an evening breeze. The greyish finger could easily be seen in the moonlight, cast by the gossamer face shining down from above amongst the shimmering stars.

Every so often, the questioning hoot of a night owl would hollowly echo throughout the trees while the crickets and critters of the surrounding woods carried on their own private earthly conversations.

It was peaceful nights like this that I strived for the impossible, seeking to recharge my batteries before the next call to action.

Nothing is impossible, dear hexed one.

I didn't immediately reply to Pearl Pippa Allifair, our resident feline familiar. Please don't be under the impression that the sleek white cat with an English accent was mine. For one, she was way too optimistic for my liking. Two, she actually belonged to Piper Allifair, who had joined me on my quest to…well, strive for the impossible.

"What's so impossible?" Orwin asked, not even bothering to look up from the laptop that was precariously balanced on his knees. He was using the mobile broadband Wi-Fi hotspot he'd set up in the RV behind us to connect to the internet. I'm pretty sure he owned every technological gadget ever created, but his very long wish list spoke to the contrary. "Can't you scoot closer? I wouldn't have to ask you useless questions then."

Orwin Cornelia was an exceptional wizard who'd also joined me in this hunt for the impossible, though he did have his own motivations that he refused to discuss in any measurable way. Throw in his amazing tech abilities and the fact that he could hear someone's thoughts from spitting distance, and he'd basically made himself irreplaceable.

You forgot to mention that Mr. Cornelia is a conspiracy theorist on the verge of wearing aluminum foil on his head. Were you aware that Minnesota has a UFO Network Blog? A sighting took place not ten miles from here, and he's been researching the witness statements for the last hour, looking for discrepancies.

"Actually, it was twelve miles, but the sighting turned out to be an elaborate hoax. They would have known that if they'd properly evaluated the witness statements," Orwin replied with a frown of disappointment, pushing his black-rimmed glasses up onto the bridge of his nose so that he could glare at Pearl. "Is someone going to answer me about whatever it is that's impossible?"

Seeing as Orwin couldn't hear someone's thoughts if they were over six feet away, I just happened to be sitting on the opposite side of the fire...approximately seven feet away. And yes, I might have done that on purpose. Between Pearl and Orwin, it was rare that Piper and I ever got a moment of privacy.

"It's not important," I replied, tucking the soft blanket underneath my denim clad legs a little tighter before reaching for the cold glass of milk I'd poured before exiting the RV. I'd also grabbed the package of chocolate chip cookies that Piper had picked up at one of the gas stations along our current route to Minnesota. The cookies weren't homemade by a long shot, but they were better than nothing when no one in our current group wanted to bake. "Go back to your blogs, vlogs, or whatever they're called so that I can eat my cookies in peace. I haven't had chocolate chip cookies and cold milk since...well, it feels like forever."

There was a reason I hadn't been able to enjoy the simpler things in life, and one of those things happened to involve the impossible I'd been trying not to discuss for the last few minutes.

You see, my name is Tempest Lilura, and I was hexed by the one and only Lich Queen in existence. At least, according to our collective knowledge.

Her name?

Ammeline Letty Romilda.

A mouthful, for sure, and trust me when I say that being cursed by an immortal witch queen wasn't an honor. Frustrating, exasperating, and downright dreadful would be more to the point.

You seem to be forgetting about that silver lining we talked about last week. I've been stocking up on those knock-knock jokes you love so much.

Only an optimist such as Pearl could find something positive about receiving graphic premonitions about impending murders.

You read that correctly, by the way.

I see murders before they happen, and my hex was putting a damper on my ability to find a spell that could remove my curse. It was also currently making it rather difficult to enjoy the simpler things in life...such as savoring my chocolate chip cookies and a glass of cold milk.

And just as a general reference, I'm not a fan of knock-knock jokes.

"They're talking about the hex," Piper offered up, having removed her headphones after overhearing Pearl continue to talk about silver linings. Either that or she just wanted one of her cookies. "Pearl is right, Lou. There's always a silver lining in everything thrown our way. If all goes well tomorrow, we might even be one step closer to finding a cure for your hex."

I set the cold glass of milk in the cup holder of my

chair, allowing me easier access to the supposedly resealable package of cookies. I'd give each and every one of them a cookie if it meant not talking about my curse for one night. Unfortunately, tearing open the seal of the package was like trying to pry tar off the highway.

Why was everything so hard nowadays?

"If you answer that question, Pearl, I'm not above throwing a cookie at your head," I warned, not in the mood for optimism or jokes. "Seriously, the two of you are liking walking beams of sunshine."

And you're the damper, Miss Lilura. It's a good thing that my sweet Piper and I decided to join you and Mr. Cornelia on this journey. Our alien hunter and I might not always see eye to eye on things, but even he deserves a proverbial day at the beach every now and then.

"I don't know how you can say cotton ball over there is a ray of sunshine when she's obsessed with etiquette. Did you know that she pushed my cereal bowl off the table this morning, all because Piper hadn't picked up her fork before I took a bite to eat?"

"That wasn't nice, Pearl," Piper chided, but clearly finding humor in the situation. Even I could hear Pearl purr in satisfaction as Piper gently stroked a hand down the feline's back. "You're lucky we had that small handheld steam cleaner in the closet or else the RV would have smelled rancid for days."

The three of them continued to talk while I went about prying open the bag of chocolate chip cookies. It wasn't that I was ignoring Pearl's advice about taking things one day at a time, but that was really hard to do with a curse flowing through my veins.

She meant well.

She really did.

Yes, I do mean well. Which is the reason I'm still awake at this bloody awful time of night, pondering over this medium we're about to go meet tomorrow afternoon. I'm thinking it would be in our best interests to research her family lineage a bit more before we expose ourselves to her divination magic.

I was so taken aback by Pearl's cautionary approach that the cookie package landed with a thud in my lap, upside down and open. She'd taken up occupancy in Piper's lap, and she certainly had everyone's attention.

I do possess a flair for gathering attention, don't I?

"What are you talking about, Pearl?" Piper asked with concern, allowing her headphones to dangle around her neck as she exchanged worried glances with us. Orwin miraculously closed his laptop, which told me that I hadn't misunderstood Pearl's apprehension at all. Oh, this wasn't good in the least. "We've been trying to meet with this woman for weeks now."

"Exactly," Orwin agreed, his glasses slipping a bit as he continued to frown. "And I've been researching her ancestry for over a month."

Which only means that a few more days won't hurt, now will it, alien hunter?

"Everything points to Cassandra Opal Saruman as being the real deal, as far as I can tell," Orwin countered with a frustrated sigh. "She's young, in college, and comes from a long lineage of witches, but that video I saw of her conducting a séance definitely demonstrates that she can talk to her ancestors."

That video only confirms for the viewer what he or she wants to see, Mr. Cornelia.

In our quest to find a cure for my hex, we'd been waylaid with various murder mysteries. Having these visions of death wasn't easy on me, and what made it worse all too often was not arriving in time at our destination to save the victim I saw murdered right before my very eyes. The gang understood that I didn't have it in me to just allow a guilty person to walk free, so we always took time away from our hunt for a cure to give closure to those victims I'd seen in my visions.

I'd had a reprieve this last week, and I was grateful for the small break. Experiencing those premonitions was quite exhausting—mentally and physically.

As well you should be grateful, Miss Lilura. Your brief respite will also allow us to do a bit more digging into Ms. Saruman's family, as well as the young girl herself.

"I don't understand." I sat up a little straighter in my chair as I cleaned up my mess, shoving the cookies back into their package. I quickly finished my task so that I wouldn't miss any pertinent facts regarding Pearl's hesitance regarding the witch we'd tracked down last month. It was rare that Pearl wasn't on board with one of our plans. "Are you aware of something that we missed?"

Let's just say I have a bad feeling about this. Don't you

think that Ms. Saruman was a little too easily found during Mr. Cornelia's search for a medium, a gifted witch with the rare ability to speak with the dead? It's a little too convenient. I mean, who puts up a video of a séance for all to see at the exact time you're in need of one?

"Practically every Millennial and Gen Z on the planet uses social media," Orwin answered Pearl, leaning back in his chair as he regarded us with annoyance over the fire. He'd searched high and low for a witch who could speak with our ancestors, even creating a database to comb every aspect of the internet for the slightest hint of someone with the required extraordinary powers who still existed on this earth. He'd been successful, too. "Pearl, I'm telling you that this Cassandra is the real deal, if one ever existed."

"Pearl wouldn't be warning us if she didn't believe her intuition wasn't a valid concern," Piper cautioned, not that she had to express her belief in her familiar's abilities. We were all aware that Pearl was a vast repository of wisdom, which far surpassed our own. After all, she'd been on the face of this earth for well over two thousand years. "Orwin, you and I can do a bit more research in the morning. We don't meet with Cassandra until two o'clock tomorrow afternoon. Let's face it. Once we found her and confirmed her lineage, we did get delayed with the whole werewolf case in Wyoming. What if we missed something?"

I would appreciate you diving a little bit deeper into Ms. Saruman's past, my sweet Piper. Doing so will ease my worries that we aren't being made fools of by a YouTube video posted on someone's social media account. My heavens, what is this world coming to?

While Orwin and Piper were digging more into Cassandra Opal Saruman's past, I guess I could take drive to the local college in the morning. Before the course of my life had been so greatly altered by my random encounter with the heinous individual who bestowed a horrible hex on me, I'd once taught psychology at a community college in the state of Washington. Not even a year had passed, yet I could barely remember what a normal day had been like in my life as a teacher.

Anyway, at least I had some type of excuse to visit the local campus where Cassandra was living the dorm life with her best friend. Maybe I could get a sense of who she was as a person, what kind of friends she had in her life, and determine if she'd maintained close ties with her coven. We didn't need to run amuck with another group of witches.

Upon further inspection, maybe that is what currently has me at odds with Ms. Saruman. The college girl's surprise at successfully conducting a séance and putting on social media for all the world to see tells me that she's either reckless or foolish. I don't care for a person to be either the former or the latter, Miss Lilura.

"It looks as if I'm interrupting something."

The deep rich voice that was like smooth molasses came out of the darkness, but I'd already caught Pearl lifting her head and twitching her nose in the direction of the woods to the east of us. She only ever did that when someone or something was near our vicinity that warranted a second sniff.

In this case, it was Knox Emeric.

Mr. Emeric's particular odor is not one I favor, if you must know. Clearly, I'm not fond of wet dog.

I was grateful in this moment that Knox couldn't hear Pearl's thoughts. Only witches and warlocks had that distinct pleasure.

Do I detect a hint of sarcasm, dear hexed one?

Out of everyone currently around this campfire, Knox was the only other one who understood exactly what it was like to be cursed by Ammeline Letty Romilda. You see, he also had a hex placed on him by the Lich Queen. If we were rating hexes, he'd win hands down.

You see, Ammeline Letty Romilda had cursed him with lycanthropy, and not just the run of the mill kind. You see, he had the greater and more malicious variety.

That's right.

Knox Emeric was a werewolf.

A very large one, of the *Canis Lupus Occidentialis* strain.

Unlike myself, who had been born a witch and had always known the supernatural realm existed, Knox had been nothing more than an average veteran going about his life. He'd mentioned before that he'd been a former active duty military special operator turned part owner of a high-end private security systems and consulting firm. He'd had everything going for him with only a bright future ahead.

Perhaps that is why I don't mind being in Mr. Emeric's presence. I mean, I'm sure that he would have chosen a lion or a leopard over a werewolf, if he'd been given the choice.

Nothing could have prepared Knox for that fateful hiking trip he'd taken into the woods...only to come face to face with an immortal Lich Queen.

I didn't realize that we had the time to share scary stories around the campfire, Miss Lilura.

"Pearl was just informing us that she thinks this medium we're going to meet tomorrow might not be on the up and up," Orwin shared, his knee bouncing up and down with agitation now that a wrench had been thrown into our plans. I knew him well enough to know that he wouldn't be sleeping tonight now that doubt had managed to creep in. He'd spend every second on his computer using the software he'd created for just this purpose—doing a thorough background check on our target. "I'm going to go make a pot of coffee."

Would you like to warm me up a spot of cream, alien hunter? The lactose does wonders to calm me in these challenging situations.

It wasn't surprising that Orwin sneezed as he passed by Knox, considering his allergies to pet dander. Piper had been bestowed the gift of healing along with her witchcraft ability, but Orwin had once again refused to lower the spell of protection he'd warded himself with after witnessing what had happened to me firsthand. Of course, that meant a constant supply of over-the-counter allergy medicine was kept on hand inside the RV.

Knox was part of our merry band of mystery hunters, as Pearl had dubbed us a while ago. I don't believe it had so much to do with solving the murders in my premonitions as much as it did with his own personal vendetta against Ammeline Letty Romilda.

I don't blame either one of you, especially considering that we're not just seeking her for the cure to both of your hexes. It is well-documented that the immortality she has cast upon herself will likely cause her to eventually go insane. In conclusion and in combination with her extraordinary power, that is not good for any supernatural being.

Regardless, Knox was a part of our group now and had informed us earlier that he was going to do a bit of reconnaissance of the small town we were visiting north of the Twin Cities. He didn't travel with us in the RV, and his decision to do so had nothing to do with Orwin's allergies.

Do you think perhaps it has to do with the aluminum foil hat inside Mr. Cornelia's desk drawer?

Just so you all know, Orwin did *not* have an aluminum hat tucked away somewhere inside the RV.

Are you sure about that, dear hexed one?

Knox simply liked his space, and I couldn't blame him. He seemed solitary by nature, and this whole thing of being turned into a werewolf had done a number on his senses. Werewolves had always made me rather uneasy, but there was something deeply inherent in Knox's character that had me lowering my guard.

I shot Pearl a warning glance, knowing that she'd completely take my thought out of context and twist it to imply some romantic connotation. Trust me, I didn't have time for such nonsense.

Are you saying that you don't believe in love anymore, Miss Lilura?

I wasn't touching that question with a ten-foot pole or an errant piece of chocolate chip cookie. Speaking of which, my milk was becoming lukewarm. I'd rather concentrate on eating than hearing any more knock-knock jokes or the reason why love existed in the first place.

Fine. We'll table that discussion for another time, but don't believe for one second you'll be getting off scot-free. I do believe there is hope for you yet.

"If it relieves any worries, there's not a vampire or another werewolf near this town for fifty miles in any direction," Knox said, claiming the seat that Orwin had given up. He rubbed his five o'clock shadow as he studied me across the top of the orange flames. "I'm not sure about any other supernatural beings in the area, but at least we don't have to worry about another set of fangs."

"I might stop by the campus first thing in the morning while Piper and Orwin do a little bit more research on Cassandra before we meet her in the afternoon," I replied, very happy with myself that I'd easily defeated the packaging and was able to pull back the flap to reveal the single row of chocolate chip cookies. "Orwin has already researched Cassandra's college friends using social media, and not one of them seem to come from a family of witches. It seems like she's trying to have a life outside of her coven, and I can relate to her decision. I do understand Pearl's hesitancy when it comes to her posting the video of a séance, regardless of the fact that everyone else thought it was a harmless prank."

I would assume Ms. Saruman's parents and coven had a very strong opinion over doing something so foolish.

"Pearl, our kind doesn't have it easy nowadays with social media and all the technology around us," Piper reminded her familiar, getting a nod of agreement from Knox. He'd basically cut ties with his family and friends, with the small exception of a text here and there to let them know he was still alive. "I'm sure Cassandra was just trying to fit in, and even Orwin mentioned that the séance wasn't her idea. At least, according to the conversation before they all started lighting the candles in their dorm room."

You know my opinion of charlatans, my sweet Piper.

"I'll drive to the campus with you," Knox offered, his dark gaze dropping to the cookie in my hand. He'd have to wait his turn, because this little treat was all mine. Did werewolves even like sugar? "How close is this coven of witches that Cassandra descends from?"

Not close enough to keep an eye on one of their descendants.

"The coven resides in or around Duluth, so about an hour or more from here," Piper reiterated, just in a more diplomatic manner.

My mouth practically salivated at the delicious scent wafting from the opening in the package. The conversation continued to flow around me while I randomly chose a cookie and picked up my glass of milk. It wasn't as cold as I'd have liked, but I was going to take these few moments to enjoy something I used to do quite often before my hex.

There seems to be a lot of acronyms these days, Miss Lilura. Maybe we should start referring to that time as BMH—before my hex. It would certainly save us time and energy, and it is quite inventive, if I must say.

The cozy scent of burning wood was by far one my most favorite fragrances of the fall season, but homemade cookies came a close second. Seeing as I hadn't had those since BMH, this would have to suffice.

I had already dipped my cookie into my glass of milk when my vision became slightly blurry, immediately telling me that the inevitable was about to happen.

No, no, no.

I hadn't even gotten to take a bite of the delectable treat, but I knew enough not to fight the inescapable vision that was about to be played right before my eyes. Breathing became next to impossible as a barely perceptible ringing began to resonate in my ears. There was nothing I could do except allow myself to be immersed in the premonition.

Oh, these visions always give me the collywobbles.

Oddly enough, due to a familiar having a link to the thoughts of witches and warlocks, Pearl was about to see every detail that played out in my mind. She and I both got a little nauseated over the graphic images, and I'd never wish these visions on my worst enemy.

Oh, I don't know about that, my dear hexed one. There is one particular Lich Queen who might be deserving of such a curse.

I suddenly found myself at the bottom of a very long and winding staircase, the kind you would see in an old mansion. I'd come to know that even the most miniscule detail could be important in locating the scene of the crime, but it wasn't always easy for me to focus on anything other than the victim—in this case, an elderly woman with long silver hair and matching jewelry.

The beautiful older female was probably in her mid-to-late seventies and wearing what some would say was a Victorian-style dress, although it had a more modern feel to it. She was clearly from wealth by the way she walked and carried herself, but it was also evident something had scared her as she quickly made her way down the marble staircase.

I could see no sign of present danger, but that didn't stop the elderly woman from emitting a loud gasp of horror as she suddenly lurched forward and tumbled down the stairs to her death.

And just like that, I was back in the present with Knox kneeling in front of me.

Well, wasn't that just dandy? Those pesky premonitions always leave me a bit knackered.

The cold damp sensation that had settled in my bones was a chill that not even the warmth of the campfire could take away, but I knew that it would fade from previous experiences.

"Are you okay?" Knox was searching my gaze for some type of reassurance. He'd never witnessed one of my premonitions before, and I didn't like that he'd seen me at my most vulnerable. I know it didn't make sense, but I'd brought everyone together. I needed to be the strong one…the leader. "Here. Give me those."

Knox had taken the package of cookies from my lap, along with the glass of milk that was almost overflowing thanks to the cookie I'd dropped inside. My chest hurt from being deprived of oxygen for the duration, but my gasping breaths began to even out with each second that passed.

Where is the alien hunter with my spot of warm cream?

"Lou, what did you see?" Piper asked earnestly, knowing full well that the faster I recalled the details of a premonition, the easier it was for us to find the location. Unfortunately, it wasn't like the potential victim had given me her name and address. "I'm ready."

Would you like to tell her about the lack of relevant details, or should I?

Piper had decided that she'd use the notes application on her phone to dictate every detail I could remember from the vision. Fortunately, Pearl was able to catch sight of things I couldn't when I got caught up in the murder mystery.

There was only one problem.

Yes, dear hexed one, and I must say it's a doozy.

"What's going on?" Orwin asked after he'd opened the door to the RV, having no idea he'd joined us at the right time for the big reveal. He stepped down, putting himself within range of our thoughts. "Oh, wow. That's a new one."

Knox and Piper shared a confused look between one another, feeling a bit on the outside of what was developing.

"Would someone like to clue us in?" Knox all but demanded, still holding my elusive chocolate chip cookies. "Why is this premonition different from the others?"

You might as well get this over with, dear hexed one. Think of it like a Band-Aid. Just rip it off, and may-be…just maybe, it will make sense to us.

"An older woman was just pushed to her death down a long and winding staircase in some ancient manor house," I finally managed to say, though my confession hadn't stung like an adhesive being pulled off my skin. Pearl was right. Nothing we saw in that vision added up. I sat a little straighter so that I came across as having some bit of composure. "Either we're dealing with the impossibility of thin air suddenly shoving a woman in the back to her death or we might actually be dealing with an evil poltergeist who's taken to murder as a sideline."

On second thought, it might have been wise to keep that detail to ourselves. Mr. Emeric seems to have lost a bit of color at the thought of a resident ghost. Oh, well. We must all deal with things we do not care to imagine. Why, just look at me. I cope with living on the road with an alien hunter while hunting down the elusive Lich Queen without batting an eyelash. I should be rewarded...with a warm spot of cream, sometime in the very near future. Don't you agree, my dear colleagues?

Chapter Two

"ARE WE SURE this is the place?" Piper asked skeptically, stepping out of my red Jeep Wrangler two days after I'd had my most recent premonition of murder. We towed my baby behind the RV for purposes just like this—easier access to crime scenes and logistical support. "Lou, this place is downright beautiful and not anything like you described from your vision."

Miss Lilura, not to question your ability to use a GPS, but are you sure this is the place from your vision? I don't recall it feeling so inviting. From the inside, at least.

I couldn't disagree with Piper and Pearl more, given that the old English-styled mansion looked positively stunning in person. It reminded me of those English countryside estates described in the turn of the century novels.

Weathered grey stones rose into the sky to form a gabled manmade mountain, guarded by stoic gargoyle statues at various peaks. The main bulk of the manor was flanked on either side by massive wings at least three stories high.

Tall dark windows peered out from the walls of stone, making one feel as if he or she were being watched by the house itself. Centered at the top of an ornate, two-tiered granite entry step were two large oak doors which featured leaded glass inlays. The thick cut glass refracted rainbows from their beveled edges, giving the massive manor before us a welcoming and almost joyous impression.

'Tis hard to believe that a murder took place inside those stone walls.

The long double lane driveway had been lined with large majestic weeping willow trees that provided shade from the sun. The hundreds of acres were perfectly manicured, although the flowerbeds had been covered in preparation for the upcoming winter.

In place of the colorful blooms were yellow hay-stacks, abundant cornstalks, and various orange pumpkins that appeared to have been professionally carved. All the fall and Halloween decorations had been done very tastefully, and without any of the traditional frightening and fun props that were seen in the yards of surrounding towns.

I must admit that I'm not fond of those standard black cat decorations with their hunched backs and fur that stand on end. It causes us intellectually inclined felines to look as if we're frightened beyond belief. I will have you know that we are braver than any human on the face of this earth.

"I actually read that cats are scared of cucumbers," Piper pointed out, shading her eyes from the morning sun as she looked around our surroundings. Seeing as Pearl was currently invisible, anyone looking out from the monstrous residence would assume that Piper was talking to me. "Not that I would ever do that to you, Pearl. But I did wonder if that was true after seeing videos on social media."

No, my sweet Piper. There's not one bit of truth to that myth. We simply just don't care for certain veggies.

Personally, I loved this holiday and all the creepy and crawly things that went with Halloween…including the black scaredy cats with the big green eyes. Maybe it was because I was raised as a witch, and we had fun using the holiday to both hide and celebrate our abilities.

Tell me, my sweet Piper, does the alien hunter know about these videos?

I hid my smile, not wanting Pearl to think that I found the chink in her armor humorous. She'd take it wrong, and then I'd feel like a petty miserable human being for anticipating Orwin actually buying a cucumber to set behind Pearl when she wasn't looking…and then stepping back to wait out her expectant overreaction.

"Orwin wouldn't do that," Piper replied, though I'm pretty sure I heard a bit of hesitancy in her tone. Maybe that was due to the not-so-nice words that had been verbalized when Orwin's cereal bowl had landed on the carpet of the RV. "Right, Lou?"

I hated being dragged into the group's latest drama, especially when it involved minor squabbles between

Orwin and Pearl. Granted, those two could be down-right entertaining, but I really did value what little I had left of my life. Speaking of which…

"Let's just concentrate on the case," I said, redirecting the conversation without a hitch. I nodded toward the other vehicles parked in the circular cobblestone drive, noticing that the majority of them were luxury sedans from prominent manufacturers. There was one vehicle that stood out from the rest, but I wouldn't necessarily have called it a clunker. "My premonitions usually provide us a twenty-four-hour lead time before the murder actually occurs. Unfortunately, we are well past that window."

I'd just like to point out that you didn't divert our previous discussion without a hitch, my dear hexed one. There is definitely a hitch that we'll be discussing later this evening. Minus the presence of any provocative vegetables.

"Oh, you're in trouble now," Piper murmured as we both began to walk toward the grand entrance of the mansion. "Pearl never forgets, nor forgives getting punked."

My sweet girl knows me so well, doesn't she?

"What I know is that these vehicles have to be here for the older woman's funeral," I pointed out, wanting to stick to the business at hand. I didn't want to invade this family's private grieving process, but I needed to know if this truly was the crime scene I'd envisioned during my premonition. "Who would have ever thought that this mansion would have been located north of Duluth? I mean, that's only an hour from the campsite."

We'd wasted precious time researching the wrong area, truly believing that the murder site we were looking for had been in Wisconsin based on a picture that Pearl had recalled from my vision. Like I said, she was able to catch the slightest details while I had a very hard time looking away from the murder victim. It wasn't that I wanted to stare at the graphic and horrible deaths of those victims, but my brain wouldn't allow me to concentrate on anything else.

What a troubling hex.

Your curse certainly is a thorn in our sides, but it does allow us to help others. In this case, most likely a grieving family who are looking for answers.

Anyway, we'd had to cancel our meeting with Cassandra Opal Saruman yesterday, fully believing that we would be packing up and driving to Wisconsin. Fortunately, Orwin had been able to track down the specific picture that Pearl had described in detail and discovered that it had been painted for a woman by the name of Florence Isla Ashton…a woman who just so happened to live in a mansion that seemed to fit the place we were looking for just north of Duluth.

Ashton is a very important and affluent name in this area, if Mr. Cornelia's research is anything to go by. Did you happen to see the zeroes on the end of those numerous charity grants bestowed in the surname of Ashton?

The Ashtons' estimated net worth absolutely surpassed any amount of money I'd ever personally known anyone to have, but the upkeep on this place alone had to be astronomical.

I assume they have a large staff on hand. If we aren't dealing with the supernatural, then each and every family member, personal friend, and employee will have to go on the suspect list.

"Speaking of which, I found this amazing app that allows private investigators to put all their notes into numbered case files," Piper shared, patting her cross-body purse that rested against the front of her right hip. "It even has this handy white board where I can connect suspects to the victim, including motive. It's really cool."

We're not changing your name to Nancy Drew, my sweet. Sometimes you do worry me with your inquisitiveness.

"It feels good to help others," Piper quipped, unable to pass one of the Mercedes in the driveway without being distracted. She attempted to nonchalantly look inside, but she'd completely failed as her mouth hung open. I'm pretty sure she left a nose print on the driver's side window. "This must be Izzy's car. I see a tube of lipstick in the cup holder."

I thought you might be referring to the vanity license plate—IZZY.

Isabel Harriet Ashton happened to be the daughter of Florence Isla Ashton.

"Good catch," I muttered, not stopping until we reached the grandiose front doors. "Let's go meet the family, then."

I'd already known once the twenty-four-hour window passed that we wouldn't be able to save Ms. Ashton from being pushed down the stairs to her death, but we couldn't allow her killer to get away with murder. Unfortunately, I still wasn't sure if we were dealing with an actual ghost or just a loose stair tread.

We both know that it wasn't a loose stair tread, dear hexed one.

I did agree that the manner in which I saw Ms. Ashton falling down those long and winding stairs hadn't been a naturally occurring accident. Regrettably, money was usually the number one motive for murder, but who knew at this point? It was a very well-known fact that family members went directly to the top of that suspect list Piper had no doubt already started in that app she'd discovered on her phone.

I keep saying that technology will be our ultimate downfall.

"I sorta feel like we're intruding on their grief," Piper whispered after I'd use the large brass knocker to announce our arrival. I didn't see a doorbell anywhere alongside the frame. "I'll let you do all the talking."

I'm surprised Pearl hadn't tried to stop us from making such a visit earlier this morning. The last case we'd worked on involved staged funerals by werewolves, not that we'd known that at the beginning of the case. All of our questions would have been answered had we crashed a viewing of one of the deceased, but even I had boundaries.

It's good to know you're learning from past mistakes,

dear hexed one. This current mystery we've found ourselves in is slightly different, wouldn't you agree?

Oh, I would definitely agree.

You see, once Orwin had discovered who owned the particular painting that Pearl had described down to the golden frame, he'd discovered that the Ashton manor had been turned into a bed and breakfast years ago.

A very special kind of B&B, because it allows us entry into the mansion where we need to investigate a supernatural murder, Miss Lilura. Sometimes Lady Karma decides to bestow upon us a gift.

"Yeah, well, I'm pretty sure Lady Karma doesn't like me one darn bit."

I wasn't about to be drawn into a debate about karma when the front door of the mansion was about to be answered by either a family member or the B&B's staff. The speech we'd rehearsed on the drive here was embedded in my mind, but I practiced it one more time to make sure there was just enough despair that the Ashtons would allow us to stay in a couple of rooms for tonight.

Orwin and Knox had remained behind at the campsite, though they had every intention of joining us later this evening per the reservation that Orwin had slid into the computer booking system here at the manor. His hacking abilities had already played a large role in allowing us to investigate the B&B's website and records, as Pearl had already mentioned, but now I had to carry the ball into the end zone.

Piper and I tensed as the ornate front door began to open, not knowing what awaited us on the other side. The small crack began to widen, though I still couldn't make out anyone in the shadows. I kept expecting an eerie squeak to emit from the massive hinges, but the door was as quiet as a well-oiled gear.

It was inevitable that the rays of sunshine beaming down from above would highlight the individual greeting us, and both Piper and I remained quiet when our gazes landed on…

Oh, dear! What in heaven's name is that?

Chapter Three

"**M**AY I HELP you?"

I blinked a few times to make sure my eyes weren't playing tricks on me. I mean, the sun seemed to be oddly bright for this time of year. As fortune would have it, the golden rays weren't to blame for the fact that Ms. Florence Isla Ashton was definitely standing before us alive and as well as her age would allow.

I couldn't stop the oh-so-elusive emotion—hope— from spreading through me as the woman's slight Minnesotan accent was said with a rather patronizing tone.

This definitely had to be our victim.

Right?

Unless this is Ms. Ashton's twin, I'm fairly certain that she's made out of flesh and blood. Unless…

Pearl's astonishment at the sight of our so-called murder victim seemed to have worn off rather quickly, while I was still taking a moment to adjust to this turn of events. Orwin and I had always assumed that there was a twenty-four-hour window based on previous premonitions. For the first time in a very long time, I didn't mind being in the wrong about the confines of the curse.

There's a difference in being wrong and simply miscalculating, my dear hexed one. Don't shortchange yourself.

"We have reservations to stay here this evening," Piper said with a touch of despair, just as we'd rehearsed in the Jeep. She also must have realized that I was still adjusting to the presence of a woman I saw pushed to her death. "I'm Piper Allifair, and this is Lou Lilura. You have such a beautiful estate here, ma'am."

"I'm sorry, but you must be mistaken somehow," Ms. Ashton replied swiftly, not giving me a chance to properly say hello. She lifted an aged hand to her chest. It was then I noticed the white handkerchief clutched between her fingers. "All reservations have been cancelled due to a recent death in the family."

Oh, my! Another twist. These murder mysteries do get my heart beating so...

"I'm so sorry to hear that, ma'am." Pearl shook her head in sympathy, keeping to the script that would hopefully allow us entry. Given the circumstances and the presence of Ms. Florence Isla Ashton, it was our duty to ensure her safety. "No one called to let us know about the cancellation. You have our sincere condolences."

I'm putting this out there for my sweet Piper to include in her new app, but how are we sure that the woman standing in front of us isn't some sort of strange apparition or one of those zombies? I mean, we haven't technically seen any evidence that she's not.

For one, apparitions were usually ethereal to the point one could see through them. For Pearl to ask such a question after being on the face of this earth for over two thousand years gave me pause.

Times are *changing, Miss Lilura. One never knows what those in the purgatory can do, given enough energy.*

That certainly was a scary thought, and one that I needed to ponder on a bit longer at a later time. Right now, we needed to find a way inside this monstrosity of a mansion so that we could find the killer before he or she succeeded in his or her endeavor.

"I'm not sure what we're going to do now," Piper lamented in a soft tone that would no doubt generate a bit of empathy from the older woman. "There are not a lot of places to stay this far out of the nearest city. The only other bed and breakfast in the area is completely booked for a fall wedding."

Ms. Ashton didn't seem to be falling for Piper's sob story, which was rather surprising. It was rather strange, given how the newspapers and social media sites had gone on and on about how caring and doting Ms. Ashton was regarding her guests, friends, and family.

The woman standing before us was completely ignorant of our plight and didn't care to discuss it further. It was clear that Ms. Ashton had been about to close the door on us when a sweet voice came from somewhere inside the grand entryway.

"Aunt Faye, who's at the door?"

Aunt Faye? Miss Lilura, isn't that the name of Ms. Florence's older sister? Not twins, but the resemblance is uncanny, is it not? Oh, how this mystery continues to unfold.

And just like that, my hope evaporated into nothingness.

Remember, my dear hexed one, there is always a silver lining in that popped balloon.

"These people were just leaving," Faye replied rather dismissively, but thankfully the young woman needed to see what the situation was for herself.

Have I mentioned I abhor bad manners?

"Hello," a pretty woman in her forties greeted us, coming to stand by her aunt. Her eyes were a bit bloodshot, but she was dressed to the nines, all the way down to the ruby and diamond earrings hanging from her earlobes. "I'm Izzy Ashton. Is there something I can help you with?"

Now this dear heart was raised correctly.

"We didn't mean to intrude on a solemn family moment," I replied, now that my shock had faded. I'm not usually thrown off balance. Honestly, I'm not sure what my problem was today. "We had reservations for this evening, extending out for a few days. We never received a cancellation notice, but we've just been informed that there was a death in the family. We're so sorry for your loss."

Very well said, dear hexed one. There's hope for you yet.

"Please, come inside while we sort this out." Izzy shot

her aunt an unyielding stare that all but told the older woman to move aside and let her conduct business. "Aunt Faye, I'll handle this."

Ah, now things are beginning to make a bit of sense. For a brief moment, I thought we might be in some time warp created by Ammeline. I wouldn't put it past her powers, you know.

Orwin had done enough research to give us the basic facts on the Ashton family connections, but Piper and I hadn't stayed long enough to get in-depth details. We also hadn't had time to piece together a family portrait album.

As it stood, we'd already whittled away close to forty-eight hours, which was well past our window of saving the victim. Had we waited a bit longer, we might have been better prepared to handle the similarities between the Ashton sisters.

We did know that Florence also had a daughter and a son, respectively named Izzy and Joshua. The manor did have a regular staff, as well, although Orwin had sent that information to us in a follow-up email that we'd yet to open.

Piper gave an exclamation of awe underneath her breath as we finally crossed the threshold. We were both from fairly modest backgrounds by comparison, so the astonishing sight of such an affluent mansion was breathtaking. The various statues, art, and antiques had been carefully positioned for the guests to appreciate.

You would have enjoyed the time I spent in the pyra-

mids with my sweet Cleopatra. Such splendor! Material items are just that, but there are definitely some very precious objects that deserve our admiration.

Unfortunately, my attention wasn't on the marbled statues, the expensive framed art, or the marbled pillars. I simply couldn't stop staring at the long and winding staircase that was spread out before us with a rather large chandelier that could only have been made with a massive collection of the finest Baccarat cut crystal I'd ever seen. The hint of turquois fire within the individual crystals was unmistakable. It had to be an artifact straight from the Museum of Baccarat in Paris.

Let's just say that it wouldn't surprise me if it was the real McCoy.

My sweet Piper already put down money as a motive in that spiffy app of hers. It is possible that one of the Ashton heirs rigged a wire or something on the upper landing to cause Ms. Florence's horrific fall.

The not-so-gentle nudge that I got from Piper told me that I'd been gawking too long at the very spot where the victim had been pushed to her death.

No worries, dear hexed one. No one seems to have noticed your lapse of attention.

"Please forgive my Aunt Faye," Izzy replied with slight mortification, walking past the very spot that Florence had most likely been found sprawled dead in her gorgeous Victorian dress. Izzy's heels clicked loudly in the pristine marble foyer. "She's grieving the loss of her sister. Oh, who am I kidding? The two didn't really care for one another too much, and Aunt Faye isn't what you would call much of a people person. I should never have left her in charge of canceling the reservations. Joshua said he'd double check, but I didn't want him dealing with…"

Oh, dear.

Izzy's voice faded, but not before she'd begun to speak really fast and in a strained manner that signified she was ready to break down in tears. Within seconds, she'd covered her face with her hands and began crying uncontrollably.

Would one of you please console this poor woman and offer her a tissue? This just breaks my heart.

"There, there," Piper consoled, wrapping an arm around Izzy as they continued to walk past the long and winding staircase to a small enclave that had been turned into a high-top wooden desk with ornate keys hanging from antique wrought iron hooks. Had I not been so focused on the two women, I might have missed the slight sliver of energy that was no doubt created by Piper. "Loss of a loved one is never easy, but we can take solace in what they loved the most. I take it that your mother was the one who passed away? I read up on her childhood home here at the manor, and she sounded like an amazing woman."

Let my sweet Piper do her thing, Miss Lilura.

I wasn't so sure Piper's gift at healing should extend to taking one's grief away. I mean, I guess the pain of losing a loved one was stored in our hearts and souls, but was it morally right to interfere with the normal progression of the five steps of grief?

I do so try to keep up with your thoughts, but once again, you've detoured to the point where I've lost sight of your footprints, Miss Lilura.

I shifted in unease on my black ankle boots that Pearl seemed to be randomly talking about, noticing that there was a rather large living room off to the right. There was a man wearing a dark suit and talking on his phone while pouring himself some coffee that had been set out on a serving table near the large window overlooking what appeared to be some type of four-season veranda.

I assumed he was Florence's son—Joshua Harrison Ashton.

Joshua seemed to be arguing with whoever was on the other end of the line, but he quickly checked his reaction the moment his gaze caught Faye walking into the room. It was easy to see that she'd immediately launched into an explanation on our identities with little regard to the fact that he was conversing with someone else on the phone.

In all likelihood, both Izzy and Joshua were probably in line to inherit the manor, along with the entire estate. His body language all but screamed that he'd rather be anyplace other than here, especially the way he compressed his lips in irritation when it was clear Faye wanted him to take charge of the situation and run us off.

People grieved in different ways, but Izzy seemed more affected by their mother's passing than Joshua. It wasn't my place to pass judgment, so I gave him a small smile when he glanced our way.

I should have saved the energy.

Joshua dismissed me with a simple frown before turning his attention back to his phone call while picking up his coffee cup.

I'm sorry, dear hexed one. Can we get back to your muddled thoughts for a moment? Let me clarify something you don't seem to understand. My sweet Piper has the ability to heal, but it does not extend to emotional damage. What is this sliver of energy you say you felt a moment ago?

I quickly glanced back at Piper still comforting Izzy, who was now dabbing her eyes with the tissue Piper had found behind the cherry wood counter. They were still discussing how much Florence had loved the manor, and that her dream was to have others enjoy what she'd had since her childhood.

Pearl was right.

Piper was doing nothing but comforting Izzy like any other caring person would do in this situation.

So where had that sliver of energy come from that I'd sensed when we walked closer to the—

Oh, bollocks!

It was so rare that Pearl interrupted a thought or a verbal conversation that I immediately understood her expletive meant we were in deep trouble.

You wouldn't happen to have some unprocessed salt on hand, would you, dear hexed one?

Natural salt fresh from the sea was known in some circumstances to keep evil spirits at bay, but I highly doubted the delicious condiment would be enough to keep a bona fide poltergeist at bay—and one that happened to be standing in the exact spot as Florence Isla Ashton had been in my vision.

Chapter Four

"WAS THAT…"

Piper's barely perceptible whisper trailed off as her gaze gradually slipped from the staircase landing to Izzy, who was asking us a question about our reservation as if nothing unusual had happened. She was lifting the lid to a compact laptop on top of the desk, but I'd been so caught up in my surroundings that I'd missed half the conversation.

With good reason, my dear hexed one. I do believe we might have just encountered the ghost who murdered Ms. Florence Isla Ashton.

The spirit had disappeared from the landing of the staircase as quickly as it had materialized. Regrettably, I hadn't gotten a good look at the ethereal mist. As a matter of fact, no one outside of Pearl, Piper, and me seemed to have caught sight of the spirit at all.

Was that due to our supernatural gifts or had the apparition appeared only to us by its own design?

The latter would not bode well for us, Miss Lilura. Poltergeists gain strength the longer they remain beyond the veil and interact with beings on our side. Who knows how long this roaming poltergeist has been encased inside this manor? I have a feeling that we are not dealing with Casper the Friendly Ghost here.

"I'm not sure why you didn't receive a cancellation notice," Izzy replied, having composed herself quickly and was clicking away on a keyboard hidden from the casual viewer. She seemed puzzled at what the screen was showing, but I trusted that Orwin had gained access to their software and made sure our names were still listed as guests for this evening. "It seems that our system only sent cancellations for a few reservations, leaving three other rooms booked."

Mr. Cornelia at his finest. I do give that alien hunter credit when credit is due.

"That would be our room, along with our friends who are supposed to be arriving later this evening," I replied, feeling completely back to normal. I took a step forward toward the high-top desk, the haze of my surroundings having completely lifted with the departure of the ghostly apparition. I'm not quite sure the reasoning for that, but I was now feeling more like myself and able to take control of the situation. "As Piper said earlier, you have our deepest condolences on the loss of your mother. We'll be getting on our way to allow you and your family—"

"Nonsense." Izzy patted the tissue underneath her eyes before reaching inside the desk for what turned out to be a physical sign-in register. I have never seen one of those, expect in the movies. It reminded me of the way hotels kept ledgers back in the day. The added touch had most likely been Florence's idea, since her passion for the Victorian era was so prevalent in everything that surrounded us. Visiting this place was like stepping back in time. "My mother put everything she had into this place, and I will see to it that her legacy lives on properly. I do know that there is a wedding of a prominent local resident taking place this weekend in the immediate area, and I highly doubt that you will find a place to stay within thirty miles. As my mother would so often say— *Welcome to Ashton Manor.*"

"Ms. Ashton, we couldn't possibly—"

Izzy cut off my feigned attempt at departing the premises by bringing her finger down directly onto a silver bell, also a throwback to the olden days. The residual ringing in my ears didn't prevent me from hearing a random expletive float from the general direction of the great room. Apparently, Faye and Joshua understood perfectly the meaning behind the ringing of the silver bell.

They don't seem too pleased at our presence, but who could blame them? They are grieving for a relative, and they have no idea that we are here to help them receive closure for the tragedy of their loved one's death.

I guess in the grand scheme of things, they did have closure. Unfortunately, their closure was based on a misunderstanding.

Ms. Florence Isla Ashton did not die from tripping

and experiencing a horrific fall.

She'd been murdered.

We could easily leave this case alone to focus on the medium needed to help solve my curse, but that would mean we'd purposefully be leaving the Ashton family to deal with an evil-spirited poltergeist they had no idea still plagued their family.

My sweet Piper, make sure you update that app of yours. We now have four suspects.

Sure enough, a woman who had to be in her sixties suddenly appeared from out of nowhere. Pearl seemed to be playing devil's advocate, because a few moments ago she was all for the culprit being the resident ghost.

One should never rule out the obvious, dear hexed one.

"Please, let me do this for my mother," Izzy replied with a kind smile. She gestured toward the newest arrival. "This is Gertrude, and she will see you to your suite of rooms."

Gertrude simply nodded our way without speaking nor smiling. She'd let strands of silver weave through her hair over the years, not bothering to fight the aging process. Her shoulders were ramrod straight, and I couldn't pick up any hint as to what her feelings were regarding the death of her former employer.

Orwin's abilities would have come in handy right about now, but his capacity to read people's thoughts were just postponed until his arrival later this evening. Once he got a read on everyone in this manor, it should be relatively simple to rule them all out should the poltergeist be the true culprit.

Unfortunately, that would mean we had bigger problems on our hands. Banishing an evil spirit wasn't as easy as opening a door and pushing them through the exit and beyond the veil.

Regarding Ms. Gertrude's lack of emotion, she's simply showing her professionalism as a staff member. It appears that she does not allow her personal feelings to interfere with her job. I respect her dedication to the rules of etiquette and proper society. My sweet Piper, please move her to the very bottom of the suspect list.

"We provide breakfast and dinner, although the morning meal has already passed. Supper will be served at approximately seven o'clock this evening. We dress for dinner, as is custom. I already have your credit card on file, so your rooms are taken care of," Izzy said, sliding over two vintage skeleton keys adorned with braided silk tassels. It didn't escape my notice that she wasn't wearing a wedding ring. "Should you need anything at all, there is a phone in your room that will automatically dial down to the front desk."

Gertrude had come to stand next to the high-top cherry wood desk, clasping her hands in front of her as she waited patiently for Izzy to finish her welcoming speech. Gertrude would no doubt be a wealth of information about the manor and the grounds, as well as the Ashton family history. More particularly, their subtleties. Who better to know the ins and outs of this place than a long-time employee who was trained to pay attention to their needs?

Another employee?

"May I collect your luggage?"

Sure enough, an English-accented gentleman around the same age as Gertrude seemed to materialize out of nowhere. He was wearing a suit straight out of the Victorian era, giving himself a rather dapper appearance that matched his proper English. I highly doubt the erstwhile style is what he would have chosen as his own. With that said, he was the epitome of a distinguished gentleman.

"This is our concierge, Wilbur," Izzy introduced, her attention being pulled in two directions now that Faye had decided it was time for her to voice her impression regarding Izzy's decision to allow guests to stay in the manor just two days after Florence's death. "I'll leave you in Gertrude and Wilbur's capable hands, and please enjoy your stay at Ashton Manor."

I could get used to a place like this, with the exception of Ms. Faye and Mr. Joshua. I'd slot them in between the poltergeist and Ms. Izzy, leaving Gertrude and Wilbur to remain last on the list.

Izzy had practically marched toward the great room, turning only briefly to close the French doors in order to obtain a bit of privacy. She was out of luck in that department, because Faye's objections to our reservations could easily be overheard. Joshua seemed to allow his aunt to speak for him as he continued with his phone call in the background.

"Wilbur, thank you so much for helping us with our luggage," Piper replied with a bright smile, feigning ignorance. She held out her hand for me to give her the Jeep keys. I wasn't too keen on allowing someone unfettered access to the interior of my baby, but we'd prepared for this eventuality and removed every hint of magical items from the back to the RV. Thus, there was no reason for me to be rude and decline Wilbur's offer. I reluctantly held them out for her to take. "Would you like me to accompany you?"

"That won't be necessary, ma'am." Wilbur took the keys with a slight bend of his waist, before straightening to address us once more. "I will see to it that your bags are brought to your room."

Without another word, Wilbur turned on the heel of his black dress shoes and headed for the front door. Gertrude quietly reached for the vintage skeleton keys before holding them out to each one of us to take. We accepted them, and she just as silently turned around in order to lead us up the long and winding staircase.

"How long have you and Wilbur worked here?" Piper asked, sidling right up next to the older woman without any hesitation. She didn't seem the least bit worried that we might run into the apparition we'd previously seen on the landing. "Lou and I are in town to research the history of Ashton Manor, as well as other older preeminent properties in the state of Minnesota.

We're doing a written documentary on several older family homes, actually. Unfortunately, there's only so much information available online. Seeing as there's no better research then speaking to those who have lived here, I'd love a chance to sit down with you and Wilbur, if you have a moment to spare."

"My husband and I have worked for Ms. Ashton for well over thirty years." Gertrude began to ascend the staircase with ease. I guess if I'd done this routine day in and day out, my muscles wouldn't begrudge me the climb, either. "It's truly a shame that our tenure here is coming to an end."

I kept waiting for Pearl to jump in with a witty comment or two, but I hadn't heard a peep out of her since we'd left the large foyer.

I'd gotten used to Pearl being next to me as I sorted through my thoughts, but I couldn't allow her brief absence to deter me in any way. The sooner we solved this murder mystery, the quicker we'd be able to focus on the hexes still currently plaguing Knox and me.

I studied Gertrude from behind, not catching the slightest hint that she was aware of what had truly happened to her employer. Had the poltergeist been a resident of the manor for some time, it wouldn't surprise me if Gertrude and the other members of the staff had noticed odd things occurring in various rooms over the years.

"I'm sorry, I don't understand." Piper quickly

glanced over her shoulder to make sure I was tuned into their conversation. "What do you mean your time here is coming to an end? It sounded as if Izzy was planning on keeping the manor open, as was her mother's wishes."

It turns out that Ms. Izzy is not as sweet as she has led you to believe, my sweet Piper. I stayed behind to listen in on her conversation with the others, and that woman has a profound greedy streak running through her soul.

Pearl had rejoined the group just as the next step landed us in the exact spot that Florence had been pushed to her death. It was common knowledge that the surrounding temperature of a spirit tended to become quite frigid, but there was no residual chilliness in the air to signify what we knew to be true—a poltergeist resided within the walls of this mansion.

It turns out that Ms. Izzy had a motive for allowing you to keep your reservation, dear hexed one.

"I apologize. I shouldn't have spoken out of turn," Gertrude said, continuing up the stairs without making sure I was directly behind them. The brief respite allowed me to slow my pace, giving me time to scan the landing. The runner was a plush carpeted Victorian style design laid over a polished hardwood floor, and it showed no signs of tampering—not that I thought there would be evidence left behind by a ghost or any other malcontent at this juncture. "Ms. Ashton was very good to us during our time here. If you're interested about the history of the manor, you'll want to spend time in the family library. The material of the family's history is quite vast."

I didn't miss the slight Gertrude had bestowed upon the rest of the Ashton family. She'd mentioned that Ms. Ashton had been good to her and Wilbur, but she'd intentionally made no mention of the other family members.

Did you hear Ms. Gertrude apologize for speaking out of turn? Now that is a woman who was raised with proper manners. The Ashton children must have had a different role model to watch over them during their formative years, especially after hearing that Ms. Izzy didn't want to leave the manor tomorrow morning.

Pearl had lost me with the recount of the discussion she'd overheard while remaining behind in the great room.

"The family won't mind if I read through the journals and history books that recount the Ashton lineage?" Piper asked, continuing to walk side by side with Gertrude as we continued to climb to the second story of the manor. There were family portraits interspersed with expensive art hanging on the wall, each with their own lighting in the form of an overhead brass lamp. "I can only imagine how difficult this time is for them. For you, as well."

I discovered that Ms. Izzy and her brother were to vacate the premises first thing tomorrow morning, as per Ms. Faye's wishes. Ms. Florence's sister seems to believe that she holds sway over what happens here until the will is read. There was a lot of fingerpointing, but Ms. Faye has now insisted that Ms. Izzy and Mr. Joshua stay until the guests vacate the premises.

"If you don't mind me asking, who will inherit the manor now that Ms. Ashton has passed on?" I asked, taking the last step to the second story. Faye's belief about being left in charge of the estate should be easy to confirm. "Her children, maybe her sister, or possibly all of them?"

I hadn't realized that the heavy wooden railing wrapped around in a complete circle, allowing those with rooms on this level to have a perfect view of the stairs and half the grand foyer. I'm sure the guests who'd been staying here at the time of the murder had been asked to leave, but that didn't mean someone hadn't witnessed Florence's so-called accident.

A simple spell should answer that question.

"I wouldn't care to speculate on that, miss. It wouldn't be proper."

Oh, it is absolutely true that Ms. Faye believes she will inherit the manor and all of its contents, leaving her niece and nephew out in the proverbial cold. Have I mentioned my intense dislike for that woman?

"Here is your room," Gertrude announced, stopping in front of a cherry wood door with a gold-plated number three positioned directly at eye level. She unlocked the door with what appeared to be a master key and stood to the side. "Wilbur will be right up with your bags. In the meantime, you have access to the entire manor…with the exception of the other guest rooms, and of course, suite thirteen."

Isn't that an interesting twist?

"Should you need anything else, please use the rotary phone on the desk. It will ring directly down to the front desk," Gertrude continued to explain, giving us a speech that she'd probably given nearly every day for many, many years. Considering no one was currently stationed at the front desk, I did wonder who would be answering our calls should we need extra towels. "Enjoy your stay at Ashton Manor."

I'll just pop right on in to room thirteen. I shan't be but a moment.

"Gertrude, may I ask you one more question?" Piper inquired as she tucked a blonde curl behind her ear. The innocent gesture was probably what had Gertrude nodding her agreement. "A lot of these old estates are said to be haunted, but I didn't see anything online about Ashton Manor to indicate such a legend exists. You've lived on the premises for most of your adult life. Has anything like that ever occurred here?"

Gertrude didn't say a single word, and I found myself holding my breath for some type of reaction. If she gave an affirmative answer, we'd be able to quickly rectify this sticky situation and be on our way. I had no idea what we'd do if she claimed never to have heard of such a tragedy occurring within the walls of the manor. The one person who knew the truth was no longer with us. I wasn't so sure that the other family members really cared about their ancestors, given what I've witnessed thus far.

"As I mentioned before, you'll want to check out the family library," Gertrude responded, not giving us an answer to our question at all. "Enjoy your stay."

Piper frowned in annoyance that her question had been ignored. She scowled down at the skeleton key in her hand, carefully turning it over in her fingers to examine its pattern. Neither one of us spoke until we were inside the room and the door was closed behind us.

"Gertrude knows something," Piper immediately said, as if the words had bubbled over until she couldn't take it anymore. "These keys all look the same. I imagine anyone could use their own key to get into any of the guest rooms. Pearl, are you back? What did you find in room thirteen?"

While we waited for Pearl to respond, I took in our surroundings. I should point out that entering the suite of rooms was like being taken back in time.

Each room in the suite had its own natural gas hearth. The English hardwood paneling was typical of the eighteenth-century style manor house. The common sitting rooms had Queen Anne style furniture and large Oriental area rugs covering the dark polished wood on the floor.

The Tiffany lamps were sitting on marble-topped antique end tables on either end of the sofa. A small library of leather-bound gilt-titled books adorned the wall along with a Victrola positioned on a small library table with a collection of phonograph records.

On the other wall was a small built-in bar consisting of a virtual cascade of decanters and its own serving table with several glasses next to an ice bucket. The decanters were filled with a variety of dark-hued liquors.

There were two additional chairs flanking either side of the sofa, centered in front of the fireplace. A coat of arms dominated the main flourish over the hearth. The beautiful oil paintings on the walls displayed a countryside one only needed to look out the window to witness for oneself.

Centered on either wall opposite each other were two open, heavy double doors leading to the individual bedrooms. They seemed to mirror one another.

Each had its own fireplace and sitting area next to the large, queen-sized canopy beds, an antique writing table, and two separate chests of drawers. A large mirrored triple dresser stood in the only available space left in either of the rooms. Although there were electrical sockets for our various devices, there were no televisions or any other electronic entertainment in the rooms.

This suite could easily have been plucked from any upscale hotel in the late nineteenth century New England cities, such as Boston or Providence. The furniture and accoutrements in these suites were of the finest available a half-century ago. No wonder the family was squabbling over the spoils. This manor had to be worth a fortune if pieced out to antique collectors that would quickly gobble up the scraps of the estate.

I'm back, and we might have an itsy-bitsy problem.

After having explored the suite in its entirety, I was now standing next to the window. I had carefully parted the curtain and found that the view overlooked the expansive front lawn. My Jeep was easily seen in the cobblestone driveway, the back hatch opened as Wilbur finished pulling out the two overnight cases that Piper and I had both packed before we left the RV back at the campsite.

"What itsy-bitsy problem?" Piper asked cautiously as she lifted her cross-body purse over her head to set down on the antique desk that held an old rotary phone under the opposite window. Pearl had now shown herself to be occupying one of the sitting chairs, where she sat regally in her usual form. "Please don't tell me that there is a body in that room."

Not quite a body, my sweet Piper. Although the object in question could result in one...depending on your particular beliefs.

"You lost me," I replied, dropping the curtain only after confirming that Wilbur had locked the Jeep up tight before disappearing underneath the window with our two suitcases. "What object, Pearl?"

A vintage turn-of-the-century voodoo doll, dear hexed one. And before you ask—yes, there was definitely a pin stuck in the rough fabric.

"I'm almost afraid to ask," I muttered, having every intention of getting that voodoo doll in order to cast a spell to find out its origins. A room off-limits to guests that contained a voodoo doll with a pin stuck in the material wasn't a mere coincidence. "Where was the location of the pin?"

In the back, of course, Miss Lilura.

"Great," Piper exclaimed, the word dripping in sarcasm. "Someone got ahold of a voodoo doll and somehow ended up summoning a poltergeist to shove our victim. It's the most logical conclusion, but murder is murder. Someone went to great lengths to not get their hands dirty, Lou."

"That they did," I murmured, already beginning to form a plan together in my mind. "Once Wilbur drops off our luggage, we'll sneak into the infamous room thirteen. I do believe that dinner this evening should have some sort of entertainment, don't you?"

Orwin and Knox were slated to arrive in time for dinner, thus giving Orwin the chance to get a read on everyone's thoughts. Should we find that someone had called on a spirit to help commit murder, that individual needed to be held accountable. Voodoo dolls normally didn't work that way, but dealing with the dark elements of the supernatural was no laughing matter.

One of those knock-knock jokes I have stored away for a more appropriate time would work rather well here, but I do have reverence for the dead. So, dear witches, what is next on our agenda?

Chapter Five

"I'M NOT SURE we should even touch it, let alone have anything to do with it," Piper whispered, leaning back slightly to get a better view of the hallway in either direction. "It might be safer to stick with investigating the available suspects."

We'd managed to secure entry into room thirteen, not that it had required a lot of skill, considering the age and style of the locks. You see, Piper had the gift to heal, Orwin had the ability to read someone's thoughts, and I had the capability to move things, even small intricate objects such as tumblers through harnessed energy.

Yes, you shifted the lock by telekinesis, dear hexed one. We have no time to waste, so chop-chop. Snatch up the voodoo doll and let's skedaddle.

Pearl was being unusually impatient, but I didn't want to touch anything without thoroughly inspecting the item in question and being mindful of the consequences of touching a possibly cursed magical item.

Don't mistake impatience with wisdom, Miss Lilura. I mean, who keeps an empty room with the number thirteen on the door in a haunted manor to house a voodoo doll?

We're obviously not dealing with entirely stable people, and it's best we solve this mystery and move on as quickly as possible.

"Since when have we ever dealt with stable people?"

You're right, of course. We find ourselves enduring Mr. Cornelia almost twenty-four-seven.

It was a good thing that Pearl's voice indicated she was behind me or else she would have seen my smile. Orwin wouldn't have appreciated being likened to a murderous ghost.

I didn't compare the alien hunter to a murderer, Miss Lilura. I just questioned his mental state, which seemed only wise. There is a subtle difference. Now, could we move this along? We'll table the discussion of what you and I find humorous at a later date.

"Pearl, maybe you should go check out the staircase and make sure no one is coming," Piper suggested quietly, still focused on the hallway. "I'm not limiting that suggestion to merely people, either."

It would certainly help if we had a name to go along with this poltergeist.

"That's what I'm hoping this voodoo doll can tell us," I replied cautiously, walking slowly around the item we were currently discussing as I went through our options. Pearl had already explained to us that the room was vacant, with the exception of the handmade figure. I'd assumed she meant empty, but she had literally meant there was nothing else in the room—no bed, no matching furniture, and no knickknacks. "Gertrude knew enough about avoiding this room to warn us from entering. One of us is going to have to seek her out so we can get some background on what we're seeing here."

"Orwin," Piper proposed, wringing her hands now that Pearl had gone to check the stairs. Her anxiety seemed to have ratcheted up a level. "Maybe we should leave the doll here for the time being. We can always come back once we have more information on what to expect."

After rethinking our situation, I found myself agreeing with Piper. We shouldn't move the doll, but I did have time to cast a simple spell that would hopefully provide us with a few answers.

I tentatively stepped closer to the voodoo doll that someone had set directly in the middle of the dusty hardwood floor of the bedroom. It wasn't the handmade figure that frightened me so much as the dark magic associated with this object that could be used as a material component for such situations that had me a bit hesitant.

With that said, I'd still cast a quick spell to find out who placed the doll inside this room, along with who stuck a pin in its back. With the way Florence Isla Ashton lurched forward, the connection between this item and her death was definitely linked in my mind.

I mean, it wasn't like things could get much worse for me being hexed by the only Lich Queen in existence, right?

Sweet angel of mercy, are you all but begging to become a full-blown magnet for bad luck? You make my job rather hard to do when you're in here tempting fate…repeatedly, Miss Lilura.

"Pearl, you're supposed to be watching the staircase," Piper whispered earnestly without taking her focus off the hallway.

That's why I've come back, my sweet Piper. We need to vacate this room immediately. No time to waste! Miss Lilura, don't even think about casting another spell. We'll return this evening when everyone else has retired for the night.

I wanted to argue, because such an incantation could have easily helped us solve this murder mystery without much effort. It wasn't often we were handed such gifts right out of the gate.

That's what worries me, dear hexed one. We'll talk about this more back in our room. For now, someone is coming and it's in our best interests not to get caught in the one room we were told not to enter.

"You have a point, Pearl." I quickly made my way across the hardwood floor, trying not to stir up too much dust. The room was even void of any kind of rug. I also did my best to make sure the heels of my ankle boots didn't click too loud as I made my way to the door. "Why would Gertrude have specifically told us to stay out of room thirteen? Unless, of course, she wanted us to find that voodoo doll."

My thoughts exactly, which might have Ms. Gertrude

slipping a bit farther down on that suspect list.

Piper quietly closed the door behind us while I non-chalantly flicked my wrist, causing the lock to slide back into place. We were ten rooms down from ours, leaving us little time to make it back to the safety of our suite.

You won't make it, dear hexed one. Think fast!

I instinctively reached out and grabbed Piper by the arm, yanking her to a stop right in front of a portrait of an older man who bore a striking resemblance to Ms. Florence Isla Ashton.

"Maybe he was her grandfather," I said loudly, tilting my head to feign my interest in the painting. Hopefully, the person about to find us practically right in front of room thirteen would believe we were admiring the family portraits lining the long wall. "It's obvious from his high cheekbones and jawline that he was an Ashton. Why don't we go down to the library for a few hours? There could be a family tree we can use for the documentary."

Nice recovery, Miss Lilura, although I'm not entirely sure we gave this cover story a thorough enough vetting process. Why is it exactly that we're conducting this so-called documentary on mansions around the Duluth area?

A discreet cough had both Piper and me turning our heads in unison, both of us succeeding in acting surprised. I was quite pleased with our amateur abilities. The individual in question turned out to be the infamous Aunt Faye, who was still holding the white handkerchief in her right hand.

It was a horrible thought, but I wasn't sure if anyone

inside this manor cared that the matriarch had died or had been murdered.

I would have said Gertrude prior to the voodoo doll fiasco. Really, did the older woman believe we were daft?

"I'd like to apologize for my earlier behavior. Our family has been through a lot these past two days with the loss of my sister." Faye once again cleared her throat as she spared a glance at the painting we had feigned interest in. "My niece explained your situation. If I may ask, what is the reasoning for your documentary on Ashton Manor?"

And this is why cover stories should be thoroughly gone over enough times, if only to have a ready answer for such questions. I, for one, am at a loss and find myself in need of a spot of warm cream. Perhaps we can call on Wilbur. He seemed like a nice enough fella.

"I'm not sure this is the right time to disclose our reason for being here," Piper said, catching me off guard.

We were usually on the same page when it came to conducting these investigations, but it seemed she was sticking closer to the truth. I personally didn't think that was such a good idea, but I couldn't come up with a way to get her back on track.

My sweet Piper does keep things interesting, doesn't she?

"Whatever do you mean, young lady?" Faye asked, that perpetual frown we bore witness to on our arrival back in place. "Does this have something to do with my sister?"

She might have me a bit worried. I do so need that spot

of warm cream.

"Ms. Ashton, we are conducting research for a documentary involving hauntings. We have been visiting manors where there have been eye-witness documentation of strange sightings, and Ashton Manor happens to be one of them." Piper surprised me by stepping forward and reaching her hand out in comfort. Even more shocking was that Faye responded and allowed Piper to grasp her fingers. "We didn't want to mention the real reason behind our exploration due to the nature of your recent loss. Hopefully after the wedding guests leave the various manors and inns, we'll be able to find a more suitable place to stay and allow you the privacy you need during this difficult time."

I take full credit for what a genius my sweet Piper has become.

"I appreciate your honesty, young lady," Faye finally said, seeming to have come to a decision about us. She released Piper's hand and gestured that she should rejoin me in front of the portrait. "That was our great-grandfather, Eugene Ruthsford Ashton. Ruthsford was his mother's maiden name, and she wanted her family name to carry on in some way. It has been said many years ago that his spirit might still roam this manor, but I've never witnessed any sign of such a thing. My sister, on the other hand, swore that she could hear his wife calling for him at random times during the middle of the night. Florence was always the more theatrical one, and her flair for the dramatic seemed to bring in the guests throughout the years."

Not to mention that Ms. Florence seemed to have attracted a malevolent spirit along the way. We're assuming that the poltergeist originally became trapped here, but what if it was brought here by an object…say, such an item as a voodoo doll?

"What was your great-grandmother's name?" I asked rather innocently in order to keep the conversation flowing.

Orwin would no doubt have a complete dossier on the entire Ashton family when he and Knox arrived at the manor later this evening. Until then, it was prudent to get as many facts about the spirit we'd seen appear on the landing. Even the most minute detail could help him or her cross over to the other side.

Simply saying good riddance might do the trick, as well. One never knows until she tries.

"Ophelia Rosalyn Ashton." Faye seemed to have lost herself in the past with a blank expression as she continued to stare at the portrait until Piper and I exchanged a concerned glance. Grief was handled in so many different ways, we may have misjudged our initial meeting with Faye. "I just don't understand why Florence was so infatuated with her story. She was just a local girl who knew how to wile her wares so that Eugene couldn't resist her charms."

No misjudgment, Miss Lilura. Your initial intuition was spot on. Speaking of spot, about that warm cream…

"Getting back to the subject at hand, I do not believe that this place is haunted." Faye brushed what had to be some imaginary lint off her black dress before gesturing toward the staircase with her hand. "No use in further wasting your time, though. You're here. The family library is downstairs to the left. Follow the long hallway, past the billiards room. You can't miss it, if that is what you're actually looking for. Find what you need for your documentary, and then move on, please. I'll be closing this place to overnight guests and tourists. It never should have been opened to the public in the first place, but Florence had a mind of her own. It's our family estate, not a Motel 6."

Ms. Faye is overly confident about the content of Ms. Florence's will, isn't she? My sweet Piper, add to Mr. Cornelia's research list that he should dig a bit deeper into why Ms. Florence was the executor of the estate in the first place. It's clear that no one in the family trusted Ms. Faye to make the right decisions concerning her sister's last wishes for Ashton Manor.

"Thank you, Ms. Ashton," Piper said quietly as we both stepped to the side to allow Ms. Faye to pass us by on the way to her own suite of rooms. At least, I assumed that's where the older woman was heading as she continued to gracefully walk down the hallway. Piper stepped closer to me so that her voice didn't carry. "Did you notice that she didn't even glance at room thirteen?"

Ms. Faye strikes me as the type of woman who rarely makes a mistake. If she is the guilty party, she would never have given herself away with a simple glance, my sweet Piper.

"Wilbur barely said a word when he brought our luggage to our room," I reminded them, coming to the conclusion it was time to talk to the married couple. "Let's head downstairs and—"

Oh, dear! It seems we are about to receive a visitor.

Concern saturated Pearl's English tone with every word she spoke, but it was the hum of energy coming from behind us that had Piper and I slowly turning around in caution from watching Ms. Faye disappear into a bedroom at the far end of the hallway.

May I point out that this particular spirit seems a bit more agitated?

Our powers as witches sometimes had no effect on ghosts or those souls stuck in the living realm. That didn't stop me from harnessing energy from my surroundings and preparing myself for defense against whatever damage this spirit could do to our physical bodies.

"I can see her features," Piper murmured, taking a similar defensive stance until our shoulders touched. "Look. She's becoming clearer."

It's apparent that this spirit has spent years gathering up her strength. Don't underestimate her power, dear hearts.

The ethereal mist continued to hover at the top of the staircase, becoming more distinct by the second. If I hadn't been so concerned for our safety, I would have recognized the fact that she was beautiful. She had long black hair with her tresses falling over her shoulders, high cheekbones, bow-shaped lips, and a slender figure. The only thing I could focus on at the moment was that she was pointing at something very specific, but surprisingly not to room thirteen.

There goes my chance to enjoy a spot of warm cream.

You see, the spirit had trained her pointed finger directly at me.

Is there something you haven't told us, dear hexed one?

Chapter Six

"THE SPIRIT WE saw was definitely Ophelia Rosalyn Ashton," Piper announced softly as she gently ran her index finger over the beautiful features of the woman in a black and white photograph. "She didn't *feel* evil to me. Did she give off a malevolent vibe to you?"

"No, she didn't." I was leaning over Piper's shoulder to get a better look at the picture inside one of the many family photo albums. The library's filing system hadn't been that hard to decipher, especially considering every family-related journal and picture album was shelved by date. Photographs from the 1850s were rare due to the expense and crude processes used to create an image. The Ashton albums contained many of the earliest types of photos. "We need to find Ophelia's journal."

Is it possible that Ophelia's spirit isn't the only one in this manor? Ms. Faye did mention that her sister would hear Ms. Ophelia call out to her husband during the middle of the night. What if that were true? What if Ms. Ophelia had been trying to stop her husband from doing something horrible that would keep his soul trapped in this mansion?

"That thought crossed my mind, too," I confessed,

scanning the very top row of the bookcase. "I'm not so sure Eugene's soul remained behind after his death, though. If he were the stronger spirit, we would have already sensed him by now."

Unless Mr. Eugene has learned to manipulate his energy. Anything is possible, Miss Lilura.

The family library was ornately exquisite with the dark English walnut paneling and matching furniture. Ladders were accessible and able to be rolled to whatever section the researcher desired. The massive river rock hearth traveled up until it touched the high ceiling. Someone had seen to it that the stack of oak logs was burning steadily, adding to the warm ambiance.

The brown overstuffed leather furniture had been positioned just so around the fireplace, with antique pieces that accentuated the décor. A tray filled with a silver service tea set and another with cut crystal glasses corresponding with decanters of various dark liquors had been arranged on either side of the room, allowing the visitors to choose their preferred drink.

Oddly enough, there didn't seem to be any threatening presence anywhere in this area.

Is it possible you might have pleased Ms. Ophelia by coming in here to do your research on the Ashton family?

"Anything is possible." I'd found that out the hard way, but Piper was right about one thing—I didn't get the sense that Ophelia had been threatening us in the upstairs hallway. "Piper, would you please go check on the Ashton family? Faye retired to her room, although I assume only for a brief afternoon nap. I know it's taking a chance of getting us thrown out of the manor, but see if you can bring up the anomaly of room thirteen into the conversation. We need to find out why Gertrude would warn us against entering another room. The thought never would have crossed our minds if she hadn't mentioned it, which goes back to our original assumption that she wanted us to find that voodoo doll with a telltale pin stuck in its back."

It's also very convenient that Ms. Gertrude left the manor to go shopping at the local grocery before we had a chance to seek her out. I could only imagine that an estate this size has a regular delivery truck service. I realize that the majority of the staff would be given the week off after the death of Ms. Florence, but I would think a place like this would have a significant store of groceries and necessary items on hand, probably enough to feed a small army.

"You make a good point," Piper said, walking the photo album we'd been leafing through over to a side table so that we didn't misplace the book. She was much like Orwin with his love of anything to do with history. "I'll stick to the cover story about the documentary. Do you think they'd believe me if I said Ms. Florence was the one who initially contacted us?"

"I'd say so, given what Faye let slip about Florence hearing Ophelia cry out her husband's name in the middle of the night."

By this time, I was already rolling a ladder to the

section that would contain the personal journals from the generation of Eugene and Ophelia Ashton. Faye had mentioned that Ophelia was a local, and one who hadn't originated from a wealthy background. I could only imagine the personal accounts recorded in her journals. That is, if Ophelia had been the type of woman to pen her feelings to paper.

"Wish me luck," Piper said, quietly slipping out of the library and closing the door behind her with barely a sound.

The décor of this room reminds me of turn of the century England.

We were usually so caught up in solving these side mysteries that Pearl rarely talked about her two-thousand-year-old past.

Don't get me wrong. She had plenty to say.

She certainly provided very specific details when the time warranted, but we were always driving someplace or researching a way for me to be rid of this hex. It was kind of nice to have her as a personal resource to ask those random questions that always seemed to come to mind at the most inopportune times.

"Pearl, you mentioned that the archeologist who found you in Cleopatra's tomb took you back to England. Do you miss the Egyptian culture?"

I began to carefully make my way up the ladder in order to reach the top shelf of the bookcase. It should go on record that there wasn't a speck of dust on the shelves or any of the multitude of leather-bound books. The number might very well be in the several thousand. Whoever on staff charged with the job of maintaining the manor's library deserved a grateful pat on the back for a job well done.

I certainly miss my dear Cleopatra. She had such strong magical abilities that it used to take my breath away. England became my home, though. I spent far more years there living within one family than in any other place I'd ever been. Highclere Castle made this manor look like the servant's quarters. It was grand in a way only a historic English family holding could be. Lord Carnarvon was an earl, of course.

The wistfulness in Pearl's voice had me wishing I was a witch with time traveling abilities. I'd never met a traveler, as they were known as. They were few and far between, often keeping to themselves. Truth be known, they were quite rare, much like Piper's ability to heal with just the touch of her hand.

Lord Carnarvon's daughter was quite the handful. It's my sweet Piper who reminds me of Cleopatra's gentle soul. She always wanted to do right by her people and took her role as her people's divine leader far too seriously.

"How did you become linked with Piper?" I asked, looking down from my perch at the top of the ladder.

Pearl had materialized and was gracefully slipping in between the various antique vases placed strategically around the library. It was as if she were a slip of herself and not really here in the present time. Her thoughts had taken her back centuries upon centuries ago.

The Allifair surname can actually trace its origin back to Great Britain, and it was one of my sweet Piper's ancestors who called me forth after the passing of my dear Evelyn. She might have been a handful, but I was always able to keep her on the straight and narrow.

"I'm sure you did," I replied with a small smile. By this time, Pearl had made her way across the lower shelf of the collection of bookcases on the other side of the room. She was making her way to the one of the exceptionally tall windows located on either side of the hearth. The glass that made up the dozens of panes was wavy, making the grounds beyond seem as if they were an artist's rendering of the surreal landscape. "You've done a great job with Piper."

Sometimes I fear I've kept her far too sheltered.

I don't think I'd ever heard Pearl doubt herself before, and I found myself somewhat in an awkward situation standing at the top of the room looking down. Piper did have a tendency to be overly trusting of random people and often believed that the complicated situations we often found ourselves in would always have a way of working out for the best, whereas I was the complete opposite.

But Pearl assuming she was the sole influence responsible for fostering that innocence just wasn't the case.

"Piper grew up in a small town," I pointed out, unable to let this topic go without giving Pearl a bit of reassurance that she was still at the top of her familiar game. "From what I've come to learn, the Allifair family was and still remains quite protective of Piper. Pearl, I know that the two of you wouldn't be here if you didn't feel these cases, the ones we've had thrust upon us, wouldn't help Piper grow in some way."

Joining you and Mr. Cornelia on your journey to find a cure to your hex was all my sweet Piper's idea, if you remember correctly. Where she goes, I go.

Pearl was being modest in her ability to influence Piper, but that was expected given the familiar's demeanor. She wasn't technically modest concerning most things, but she was humble about her interactions with Piper.

"Pearl, I'll continue to do my best to make sure that Piper is never hurt during these cases," I promised, continuing to watch Pearl as she navigated around a vase filled with fresh flowers near the windowsill. "If the time ever comes when I need to confront Ammeline, I'll—"

You'll not face that Lich Queen alone, so you can dash that thought right out of your head, dear hexed one. Piper and I are now part of your traveling family, and we'll be there when the going gets tough. We just need to make sure that my sweet Piper is prepared, and cases like these will be what help fortify her arcane abilities as a witch. Now, enough chit-chat. We have much more work to do.

I did hope that Piper's gift of healing didn't need to come in handy too soon, given our circumstances. Orwin in particular was at risk due to the warding spell he'd cast over himself to protect against anyone using witchcraft on his physical being. That included healing spells and curative potions. He'd done the right thing in his own judgement, but he'd also left himself wide open to the risks of getting injured or worse…the very real possibility of death.

Miss Lilura, do I need to go through my list of knock-knock jokes to shake this avalanche of conundrums you keep making up in that thick head of yours? You worry more than Cleopatra's guards, and they were of some renown. The pharaohs were demigods, in case you forgot. They were guarded by heroes of the realm.

I pursed my lips in frustration at Pearl's attempt to get my mind off what had definitely crossed everyone's mind recently, especially after our run in with a pack of bloodstained werewolves in Wyoming. Had it not been for Knox's abilities, I'm not so sure we would have come away from that case unscathed or intact.

Focus, dear hexed one. I'm sure our time in here is limited in some fashion or another, considering that my sweet Piper is bound to get the Ashtons' strict attention once she brings up room thirteen.

We'd already canvassed the landing for any type of trip wiring or hook where a string could have been threaded in order to trip Florence to her death. No tract of anything had been found, which gave credence to the whole ghost theory.

That thought had me carefully shifting on the ladder so that I could read the titles of the leather-bound books. Interspersed between those historic items were personal journals made of soft rawhide and tread-bound yellowed parchment paper. There was no way to know which diary belonged to which Ashton, so I took care to start from the beginning of the shelf and work my way across now that we had an elementary understanding of the family's ancestry.

I became so engrossed with the research that I lost track of the time we spent here.

The Ashtons were a very interesting family, particularly Eugene Ruthsford Ashton. His was the fourth journal I'd pulled off the shelf, and I'd been standing on the ladder for quite a while. My legs began to burn from the position I'd put myself in, but I didn't want to climb down until I'd found Ophelia's diary.

You better make it quick, dear hexed one. I hear someone coming down the hall.

I instinctively reached for the leather tied journal that had tilted upon me withdrawing Eugene's accounts of his later years, clasping both in my hand as I began to carefully make my way back down the ladder. Pearl had vanished, and I had just set my boot on the polished hardwood floor when the ornate doorknob began to turn.

Wilbur? Now what is Gertrude's husband doing seeking you out, Miss Lilura? Be careful with this one. I've never had good dealings with those who have overly bushy eyebrows that practically touch the middle of their forehead.

"Miss Lilura, I was hoping to find you here," Wilbur said in a hushed tone, closing the door to the library before turning to me in earnest. He clasped his hands in worry as he stepped closer. "Is it true that you and Ms. Allifair are…to use the vernacular term…ghost hunters?"

Oh, dear. What has my sweet Piper said to the Ashton family members that has this man enamored with the idea of ghost hunting?

Wilbur had all but whispered the description, as if someone else was in the room with us. He *had* taken the time to look around the large room. I stopped myself from following his lead, wanting to take advantage of this time to ask him pertinent questions. I would have sensed a presence had Ophelia joined us or any of the other spirits that might be within the walls of the estate.

"It's not what you think, Mr. Wilbur," I explained, holding the two journals close to my chest. Izzy had only introduced Wilber and Gertrude by their first name, so I showed him deference and appropriate respect the best I could with the limited information I'd been given. "We're doing a documentary on hauntings, but we aren't actually those kind of ghost hunters like you see on television."

Humans had a tendency to make fun of the super-natural with movies, books, and television shows. What they didn't know was that they had probably run into a predator or two in their lifetime without ever being the wiser. Vampires and werewolves, in particular, hunted one another if their paths crossed. For the most part, they did their best to keep the peace where the public was involved.

It's those human hunters that worry me. Mr. Cornelia showed me a website once where those mere mortals congregate to discuss the supernatural. I'm very close to talking the alien hunter into hacking their network and shutting them down for good.

I highly doubt that Orwin would do any such a thing, but it was comforting to know that Pearl would go the extra mile in keeping those within our own realm safe from harm.

"Aren't you going to set up any of those fancy detector machines or bring in some medium who can talk to those spirits who are stuck in this place?" Wilbur asked, a rather stern frown now settling into his weathered features. "There are ghosts here, Miss Lilura. I know it. I can feel their eyes on me every time I walk into their rooms."

I'm relatively sure that Mr. Wilbur's eyebrows just grew a half-inch. Either that or it's gravity at play.

Wow. Pearl must really not like his bushy eyebrows, because she hardly ever allowed her manners to slip.

Manners? I'm simply stating the obvious truth, Ms. Lilura. Could we please speed this along? I'm thinking we can take those journals up to the room, you can order up a spot of warm cream, and we can settle in until the alien hunter and our new rescue dog show up for dinner.

"No machines, Mr. Wilbur. Just good old-fashioned research to put into the documentary. We've seen the reviews of the Ashton Manor online, and there were a few posts that spoke of that same feeling of someone watching them," I replied, figuring now would be the perfect time to ask him the questions we needed answered. "Do you know who might still be haunting this manor? Ms. Faye told us that Ms. Florence could hear Ophelia call out to her husband in the middle of the night."

Wilbur looked over his shoulder at the door, as if to double check that someone hadn't opened it without him taking notice. His blue eyes had clouded with age, but they somehow darkened even further upon talking about poltergeists.

"You misunderstand me, Miss Lilura. It's not just the ghosts who haunt this manor nor is it just the spirits who have their eyes on everyone," Wilbur murmured, leaning in close enough that I could smell the underlying scent of Old Spice aftershave. "Don't be fooled by the Ashtons."

The spirits who have their eyes on everyone? So, this older gentleman does know about the ghosts roaming the halls. This is taking a very interesting turn, dear hexed one.

I was more worried about Wilbur's warning about the Ashton family. He hadn't helped discern if the guilty party was of the living or the dead in the least. As a matter of fact, I was becoming more concerned by the second that this mystery might take longer to solve than I'd originally suspected.

"Oh, there you are," Izzy exclaimed, having come through the library door so suddenly that I was afraid Wilber would clutch his chest and fall to the floor to his death. "Wilbur, I've been looking all over for you. Gertrude is back with a truckload of groceries. Would you be a dear and go help her? With most of the staff off this week, we're a bit shorthanded in the kitchen."

"Of course, Ms. Ashton," Wilbur exclaimed, although he'd lost a bit of his color. "I was just answering some questions regarding the maze on the back property. I'll be getting back to my chores now."

Maze? It seems as Mr. Wilbur was kind enough to throw us another bone, unless that was his way of throwing Ms. Izzy off our trail.

"Ms. Lilura, please know that what happened in the maze last year was nothing more than my mother's overly active imagination," Izzy exclaimed, almost in disappointment that the subject had even been brought up. Her acting abilities from this morning were beginning to show their frayed edges. "There are no supernatural spirits or nasty ghouls roaming this manor. My mother had no one living in this big old place besides the staff and herself, and she was a bit lonely for company. Imaginations run wild under those types of circumstances."

Ms. Izzy appears a bit tense, doesn't she?

I had noticed right away the manner in which Izzy was clasping her hands together as she attempted to explain the maze incident—whatever that might be. It would definitely be added to the other twenty or so leads that Piper had jotted down in the app on her phone.

"Now, Ms. Allifair explained that Gertrude had mentioned room thirteen, of all things. I checked the renovation log," Izzy explained a bit tersely. It seems we were wearing out our welcome. "According to my mother's laundry list of needed maintenance tasks, room thirteen needs to be painted and updated."

"I'm sure the manor takes a lot of upkeep," I responded, treading carefully as I was unsure of what Piper might have said to the Ashtons. "It's noticeably well-loved, and the small details like the fire in the hearth and the hot tea make all the difference. I can see why people rave online about their stays here at the Ashton Manor. You have an impressive Yelp rating."

Very well done, Miss Lilura. I do wonder, though. Is it possible that Ms. Florence was the one who cordoned off the room for whatever voodoo ritual she was conducting? That is a theory we never explored.

Izzy dropped her gaze to the items I had tucked away in my hand. Her precious frown had now turned into a full-on grimace.

Are you sure, dear hexed one? Those Botox shots make it very difficult to come to such a conclusion without a detection spell.

"Your colleague expanded on this documentary of yours," Izzy stated with displeasure. "I'm not thrilled to discover that the focus is on false stories regarding my ancestors. Let me be perfectly clear—this manor is not haunted. Nor was it ever. With that said, I promised you and the others a place to stay this evening. I'll honor my word to do so, however, my family and I would appreciate it if you would leave after breakfast."

The mere mention of ghosts seems to have riled Ms. Izzy,

hasn't it?

"We meant no disrespect, Ms. Ashton." It seems that our investigation had just been put on the fast track, not that we were anywhere near solving Florence Isla Ashton's murder. "We'll leave after the morning meal, giving you and your family your privacy."

We will? I'm going to assume an amazing idea to find out what happened to Ms. Florence has popped into that hexed head of yours. I'm currently not seeing how we could expedite this murder mystery, but then again, I've been deprived of my spot of warm cream thus far.

"I appreciate your willingness to—"

A piercing scream broke off Izzy's reply, causing Izzy to startle and me to immediately leave the library to find out the cause.

Your fight or flight response is quite admirable, Miss Lilura.

Pearl was keeping up with my light jog in her concealed state, although Izzy had fallen behind with those heels of hers. I practically skidded to a stop when I saw Gertrude staring up at the staircase in horror while Joshua stood behind her. The pallor of their faces was that of chalk.

It's as if they've seen a ghost, dear hexed one.

Piper must have been in the kitchen with Wilbur, because both of them appeared together from that general direction. As for Faye, the loud shriek had succeeded in waking the woman up from her afternoon nap. I could hear her calling out to us from her balcony above.

"What on earth is happening down there?"

Gertrude didn't respond to Faye. She seemed incapable of talking, and she ever so slowly lifted her right arm to point a shaking finger at the same exact spot that I'd seen Florence pushed from the landing. Joshua actually took a step back, almost as if he were considering his most likely avenues of escape.

My opinion of Mr. Joshua continues to remain rather low.

"What is it?" I asked, having looked up at the landing to find nothing amiss but Faye carefully making her way down the staircase, exchanging handholds on the wooden railings as she descended at top speed. "Gertrude, what did you see?"

"A ghost, Miss Lilura," Gertrude whispered in fright, grabbing onto Wilbur's hand when he came to stand next to her. "The ghost of Ophelia Rosalyn Ashton."

I don't always like to be right, Miss Lilura. It's a curse, really. Oh, dear heavens! Did that slip out in my utter astonishment? I do so apologize for my lack of decorum, dear hexed one. On the bright side, the Ashton family will no longer be able to deny they have an entity roaming the halls of their family estate. My sweet Piper, now would be a good time to utilize that app of yours to catalog their apparent responses to the latest developments.

Chapter Seven

THE SILENCE BECAME rather heavy in the great room as evening began to set in. We were all currently seated around the massive hearth, certainly one even more grand than the one in the library. Piper was utilizing this time to our advantage, poring over the journals I'd retrieved from the top bookshelf. Everyone else had strategically taken a seat in a way that they could keep their attention on us, as if we were to blame for the spirit haunting their home.

Well, since you were the one to bring up the subject...our presence could very likely be the motive for Ms. Ophelia to show herself to the others. The woman is clearly trying to tell us something, and spirits do thrive on negative energy. We may have just provided Ophelia with enough of a current to make herself visible whenever she pleases.

I agreed that Ophelia had a message for those who remained inside the manor. Most poltergeists were envious of the living, and everyone's lives were in danger the longer they stayed under this roof.

I don't believe that Ophelia was using our energy to materialize in front of the others, especially considering that Florence had told many people she'd heard Ophelia's cries in the middle of the night. If Ophelia was responsible for Florence's death, it was safe to say that the spirit had enough strength on her own without the need to use us as a catalyst.

It is quite possible that whoever was using room thirteen to dabble in voodoo might have inadvertently harnessed enough negative energy for the ghost of Ms. Ophelia to do his or her bidding. So many questions, so little answers.

"It was very sweet of Gertrude and Wilbur to cook dinner for us tonight," I said, causing Izzy to startle a bit while Faye slid a bored look my way. Joshua was standing next to the hearth with a drink in his hand, staring into the flames with such concentration it made me wonder if he was trying to burn the image of Ophelia out of his mind. "I realize that the majority of the staff was given the week off in the wake of Ms. Ashton's death. I'm sure Gertrude and Wilbur didn't count on serving guests during this time of grief."

From the look on their faces, I don't believe that Ms. Gertrude and Mr. Wilbur have ever truly encountered a spirit while working for the Ashtons. That puts both of them back at the bottom of our list. Of course, that's based on a currently unproven assumption that the culprit conjured Ms. Ophelia's help to commit the murder.

Piper had been busy jotting notes down in that app of hers while discovering interesting facts within the journals. After Pearl's opinion on the married couple, Piper casually pressed a finger to her phone and drew it downward, most assuredly moving the suspect list around.

In case you were wondering, Ms. Faye is at the top of the list. According to Piper's constantly evolving notes, the motive is money and revenge. Piper finally got around to opening Orwin's email. Apparently, Ms. Faye had originally been left out of their parents' will, with the exception of her somewhat generous trust fund. It appears that Ms. Florence was the one to solely inherit the estate so many years ago. That creates a motive for murder.

The only way for Faye to regain control of the estate was if her sister saw fit to put her accession in her will.

"Is it true?" Joshua asked with seriousness, losing me with his random inquiry. He'd shifted on his dress shoes, still adorned in a dark suit. The phone that was usually glued to his ear had been slid into the inner pocket of his jacket. I was looking out the front window toward the drive, waiting for Orwin and Knox to arrive. "Are you and your team here at the request of my mother before she died?"

Oh, the lies we weave to get to the truth. Such a misnomer, no?

I'd never gotten a chance to speak with Piper regarding her conversations with the Ashtons, but Pearl had filled me in on a major point. Piper had gone with the fabrication of Florence reaching out to us upon hearing about our inquiries sent to other estates about the premise for our documentary, and that we were simply here to prove or disprove her theory about Ophelia.

"It's not as simple as that, Mr. Ashton," I replied carefully, not wanting to blow our cover by saying something directly opposite of Piper. "It's true that we were researching family estates in the area where hauntings were said to have occurred, and we did speak with your mother. Ms. Ashton confirmed there were unusual sightings and sounds, and we took her up on the invitation to stay here at the manor. Piper and I have yet to see any signs of a supernatural spirit for ourselves. What exactly did you and Ms. Gertrude see on the landing of the staircase, Mr. Ashton?"

Very well done, dear hexed one. Now the ball is in Mr. Ashton's court, should he choose to play.

Piper was frowning over one of the journals, and it didn't take me long to recognize it as the one that belonged to Eugene. Something of interest was in his diary, and I was hopeful it would help us figure out why Ophelia remained behind instead of crossing over to the afterlife to join him.

"I...I don't know what I saw," Joshua said rather briskly, turning back to set his gaze on the flickering flames. "It could have easily been a trick of the light. The chandelier alone can cast an array of colorful illuminations."

"What if Mother was right about this place?" Izzy asked, directing her guarded inquiry to Faye and Joshua. The sudden shift in conversation had Piper finally looking up from the journal. "What if Ophelia is trapped here? What if she's been the one—"

"That's enough," Faye snapped, interrupting whatever it was that Izzy had been about to reveal. "This manor is not haunted. I forbid it, and I will not listen to another word of such blasphemy."

"Mom said strange things have been happening here at odd hours," Izzy revealed, casting an accusing glare her aunt's way. "Are you telling us you didn't notice anything? No strange sounds? You didn't see anything unusual in all this time?"

Faye pursed her lips in frustration, clearly having no intention of answering her niece's inquiry. It did make me suspect that maybe she was the one who'd placed the voodoo doll in room thirteen, but I had a hard time believing that she'd ever consort with any type of magic.

Greed has a way of causing an individual to make some foolish choices.

Humans had no idea the damage they could produce when experimenting in something they didn't quite believe was real, yet still sought its power.

"Izzy, did you ever consider that maybe our dear aunt was the one responsible for Mom's erratic behavior toward the end?" Joshua had not only dug in the knife, but he was twisting the blade. "What if she set this entire thing in motion in order to cause this mess?"

"I did no such thing!" Faye protested, laying a hand over her heart in mortification. "I loved my sister. We'd mended our relationship over these past six months, but you wouldn't know that, would you? The two of you gallivant around with your overinflated trust funds, having no respect for the care that your mother put into this estate. You should be ashamed of yourselves!"

I'd forgotten what it was like to be in the middle of a family ruckus. They are quite entertaining, are they not? I do so remember Lord Carnarvon battling it out with his family over his obsession with Egyptian antiquities. Quite compelling arguments, I admit. It also cost him his life.

"You're only saying that, Aunt Faye, because you wouldn't be able to sell this place if word got out that the manor was haunted," Joshua countered in anger, turning to face his aunt and sister. "I still don't know how you managed to talk Mother into leaving you the entire estate. Did you use blackmail? Is that it or did you prey on her superstition?"

And now the truth unfolds itself...

"Stop it," Izzy demanded, leaning forward and slamming her drink on the ornate coffee table. "It's rude and quite unseemly to carry this conversation on amongst guests, and we only have Aunt Faye's word that Mom recently changed her will. The reading of her last will and testament isn't scheduled until Monday."

Their collective motive is certainly drying in the cement, is it not?

"The two of you can go on home until such time. I will have you know that your mother finally came around to recognizing me as the rightful heir to the estate. As such, she did have the family lawyers change her will," Faye admitted proudly, even tilting her chin in superiority. "Is it so hard to believe that your mother and I mended our relationship over these past few months?"

Piper is doing a very splendid job of keeping up with this conversation as she jots down notes in her app. I wonder, do you think this discussion will spit out the murderer when all is said and done? We'd be resorted to our position as minions simply gathering the facts of these mysteries. I've tried discussing this with the alien hunter, but he won't see reason. Mark my words—technology will be the downfall of a reasoning humanity.

"You mean the six months you stayed here because you drained your trust fund and had to rely on the generosity of the estate to support you?" Joshua accused before downing the rest of his drink. I'm relatively certain it was bourbon, but then again, it might as well have been truth serum. I'd turned down his offer of a drink, needing to keep my faculties about me after Ophelia had shown herself to the others. Seeing him start to unravel told me I'd made the right decision. "Yes, Aunt Faye. We were perfectly aware of that little wrinkle. Unlike you, our mother didn't keep secrets from us."

"She did, though." Izzy's eyes filled with tears, and she took a deep breath to try and control her emotions. "Mother didn't tell us about the will, and now Aunt Faye can do whatever she wants with the estate. What if it's true?"

They're learning that secrets have a way of destroying families. Such a hard lesson to learn, isn't it? Quite sad, really.

"I'm not leaving," Joshua exclaimed, defending his decision. He, too, slammed his empty glass on the fireplace mantle. "And neither are you, Izzy. We're going to fight the will and claim that Mother was under duress. We'll tie you up in court for decades, Aunt Faye. The first thing we'll insist upon is a court-appointed forensic accountant to analyze the books and a conservator to control future disbursements."

"You can try, dear," Faye murmured, taking a sip of the wine she'd poured herself earlier. "You can certainly try."

Piper and I had all but remained silent throughout the family fallout, for many reasons. Most importantly, this was a private matter that never should have been discussed in front of strangers. On the other hand, the motives from all three of these family members were being brought to light with every word of their argument.

I daresay that the results of my sweet Piper's app are leaning more and more toward Ms. Faye.

I wasn't too worried about any computer results at the moment, because I could clearly make out the headlights of an oncoming train. Wayward emotions, such as the ones running rampant in this manor, had a way of prompting not only accusations, but emotional outbursts. I figured it was only a matter of time before Joshua and Izzy came to the snap decision that their mother's death wasn't an accident, as it had been portrayed. They would be partially right, but had Faye been the one to cause Florence to fall down those stairs?

Recalling the premonition I'd endured two nights ago, I wasn't so sure that was the case.

Dear hexed one, Mr. Joshua and Ms. Izzy would inadvertently be right if we discover that Ms. Faye was indeed the one to use a voodoo doll to conjure up the ghost of Ms. Ophelia to do her bidding.

The only way we'd ever know who utilized the voodoo doll for his or her own gain was if we spoke to the one entity who would have either witnessed the magic itself or been called forth to carry out the horrific deed. After all, casting a spell on a voodoo doll could technically backfire quite easily. The last thing I needed was more carnage in my life. So that currently left us only one route, unless Orwin was able to pick up the murderer's thoughts. Easier said than done, if Ophelia's spirit was indeed the true killer.

You're not suggesting…

Pearl's incredulity over my internal thoughts had Piper swinging her startled gaze toward me, but I'd already made my decision—we were going to have a séance.

Oh, dear!

Chapter Eight

"WELL, THAT DINNER didn't go quite as expected," I said to Piper wryly, having stepped outside after receiving a text from Orwin that he and Knox were about to pull up the long winding driveway of the estate. "It looks like we're resorting to plan B."

Our two colleagues had run into an accident on the highway that had them at a standstill for several hours. We'd already endured the evening meal, where Izzy had all but rushed to her room after Gertrude emphatically denied that the apparition she'd seen on the staircase landing had been a trick of the light reflecting off the chandelier.

Needless to say, Joshua and Faye had immediately gotten into another heated argument about the manor being haunted and how that may have contributed to his mother's demise. Wilbur and Gertrude very openly announced their joint resignation after dessert was served. I wasn't sure if their decision was due to what Gertrude had witnessed on the landing or if they couldn't take any more of the Ashtons' bickering over the ownership of the material wealth of the estate.

By the time the dishes were cleared and all was said and done, Joshua had retired to the great room for another tumbler full of whiskey while Faye was frantically calling some of the other staff members to see if they'd come back to the manor immediately.

I highly doubt that Ms. Faye will succeed in her endeavor, even if she manages to contact anyone.

"I'm not worried about making myself a bowl of cereal in the morning," Piper replied in concern, rubbing her arms up and down as she began to walk beside me. I could already see the headlights of Knox's Land Rover weaving through the weeping willows. "Do you really think carrying out a séance in a place that we know one hundred percent has at least one spirit roaming the hallways is a reasonable idea?"

Not without a spot of warm cream, my sweet Piper. I need to be relaxed before we take on such an undertaking. Seeing as the kitchen is now open to guests, I'm sure you'll have no issues heating up a warm cup of sanity in the microwave for exactly twenty-one seconds.

"Not at all," I replied honestly, having every intention of obtaining that saucer of warm cream for Pearl. We needed all hands on deck tonight. "But it's a heck of a lot better than casting a spell on a voodoo doll that was possibly used to conjure a murderous spirit."

I'm not sure I covered the difference between the different magics, but I'd like to go on record as saying that voodoo isn't exactly bad nor dark in its nature. Not in the least, and I've known several witches over the years who practiced in the art that were better men and women than myself.

Any magic was capable of being used to do good or evil.

Very well stated, dear hexed one.

It's the person casting such spells that steer the direction of what humans would refer to as karma. Consequences came when using magic for self-gain or to intentionally hurt someone else. Intent mattered.

You realize this could explain why Ammeline Letty Romilda is slowly going insane over the course of her immortality. I'll have to discuss this talking point with Mr. Cornelia at length.

"I'm still hoping that Orwin will be able to walk into the manor, get a fix on everyone's thoughts, and quietly let us know who killed Florence Isla Ashton," Piper said optimistically, which wasn't surprising.

Unfortunately, Orwin couldn't read the minds of lost spirits. Especially if Ophelia had indeed committed the murder without any prompting by other family members.

Doubtful, Miss Lilura, given the voodoo doll currently located in room thirteen. Although, hearing you spout optimism is a nice change of pace.

"Don't get used to it," I grumbled, unable to prevent a shiver as the cool night temperature seemed to drop a degree further. I'd left my black leather jacket up in our room, thinking we'd only be outside a few minutes to meet the rest of the crew. "Here they come. Finally."

In cases like these, we usually had to split our resources. We each had our own talents to contribute to each case, but Orwin's ability to read minds was a top shelf tool in our recent endeavors to combat evil.

True, although I could do without all the conspiracy theories he spouts every morning over coffee. I really only indulge him because he's the first to arise every morning, and I've trained him well in my breakfast preparation routine.

"I know this sounds a bit creepy, but Orwin could always stand in front of the Ashtons' bedrooms to see if they are close enough on the other side of the door for him to pick up on their thoughts."

My sweet Piper, this manor was creepy the moment we found an empty room marked with the number thirteen containing a voodoo doll that had been stabbed in the back. Adding a conspiracy theorist creeping around the hallways attempting to listen in on the family's thoughts won't change that.

"She has a relevant point," I said with a small smirk. "See, Pearl? I don't need a knock-knock joke to smile."

That's not a smile due to enjoying the little things in life, Miss Lilura. That's amusement at my witty repartee. The fact that you've confused the two tells me that I have my work cut out for me.

The strategically placed lighting throughout the grounds of the estate, in particular the illumination the cobblestone drive, led to me catching sight of Orwin gazing at the manor in the same awestruck way we all had. His jaw was slightly ajar as he took in the mammoth extent of the main house and the front two wings. Knox, on the other hand, made direct eye contact with me.

I dare say that the temperature might have risen a couple of degrees.

I didn't bother replying to Pearl's quip. All my denial would have done was give her the idea that she was onto something in regard to my work relationship with Knox. We had a common denominator, that's all. We'd both been hexed by the same Lich Queen, and we both had a stake in finding a cure to our dilemmas.

You keep telling yourself that, dear hexed one.

Knox had pulled his Land Rover parallel to my Jeep, cutting the engine. It didn't take long for both men to step out of the vehicle, though Orwin's focus was still glued to the massive granite blocks that comprised the mansion.

"Uh, Lou?" Piper nudged me in the side with her elbow. "I don't remember the exterior of the house looking like anything but the typical wealthy estate, with a rather mundane display of fall decorations. I can see now why Ms. Florence didn't feel the need to add in the ghouls, bats, and black cats to the theme."

Sure enough, the exterior of the manor had a completely different vibe than it had this morning. The evening lighting accented the size of the surrounding towers. The gargoyles were that much scarier at night.

I hadn't realized it then, but there were candles—probably electronic—in each window that faced the front of the property. The hundred-year-old trees surrounding the circular drive seemed to loom over the eaves of the roof as if each tiny limb was like fingers reaching out to pluck the manor from its place in the grounds. Shadows lurked over the façade as if they were mere puppets on a string, every so often drifting over the edge of the windowpanes to scratch out a warning.

Truthfully, those slight obscurities made a person question if the house wasn't somehow alive in its own way.

"I'm all for taking one for the team, but do you really think it's safe to stay here?" Orwin asked, coming around the Land Rover to stand beside me. Knox had joined us, but he used the bumper to lean against as we all took in the menacing sight before us. "Our type of magic doesn't necessarily guard us against ghosts and ghouls, if you get my drift. I'm fine with sleeping in the Land Rover. How about you, Knox?"

Wait until you hear about Miss Lilura's grand idea to host a creepy séance.

Orwin didn't bother to reply to Pearl's statement. Instead, he gazed at me in horror. The fact that he'd lost all color in his cheeks had Knox's gaze bouncing off each and every one of us, trying to discern what words had just been exchanged.

"I clearly missed something," Knox replied knowingly, his rich voice cutting through the tension like it was butter. I'm pretty sure his brown eyes glowed a bit more golden at the assumption that I was the topic of discussion. "What did you go and do now?"

Mr. Emeric is getting to know you rather well, isn't he?

"I plan to solve this case by morning," I stated firmly, not backing down from the proposed plan. "Unless Orwin can get a read of guilt on one of the family members or staff who are currently inside the manor, then there would be no reason to have a séance. We'll find another way to give Ophelia some peace, if it turns out she's not the reason Florence was pushed to her death."

"Lead the way," Orwin insisted, not giving anyone else a chance to respond to my decision. He didn't even bother to gather his overnight bag. He pushed up his black rimmed glasses in determination. "We are not doing a séance within a mile's distance of an agitated spirit. Whether or not this Ophelia had anything to do with Florence's death, opening a portal for her to climb through is a bad, bad, bad idea, Lou."

Don't think this gets you out of indulging me with a spot of warm cream, Miss Lilura. I've had a rather trying day.

"I don't understand." Knox's exclamation brought everyone to a halt. Piper and Orwin had already taken a step toward the front entrance, but they both turned around when Knox made no attempt to move from his spot on the bumper. As a matter of fact, he had his arms crossed over his chest as if he were settled in for a while. "If Ophelia is already haunting this place, then hasn't she already crossed through some type of portal?"

I forget that Mr. Emeric didn't emerge from a supernatural family. His curse of lycanthropy shouldn't cause a problem, though.

If I tried to explain to you the resonance that practically vibrated the ground under our feet, I probably couldn't do it justice. I'd lived for many years on the West Coast and experienced many earthquakes of various magnitudes, but this sudden blow from out of nowhere was unlike anything I'd ever experienced.

Orwin's glasses had been left askew, and Piper had grabbed ahold of his arm. She did so more out of fright than need.

"What the—"

Hades. Tell Mr. Emeric I don't appreciate curse words, and he will have to find more appropriate expletives. I will not hear such filth on the day we might possibly be swallowed by a hole in the Earth. Speaking of which, why isn't there a hole underneath us at this very moment?

The only reason Knox had cut off what he'd been about to say was that Pearl had abruptly materialized on the spare tire hooked to the back of the Jeep. He hadn't heard Pearl's reprimand, but her sudden appearance had caught his attention.

You realize that this day has continued on a downward spiral all due to my deprivation of cream?

"That wasn't an earthquake," Piper whispered as we all cautiously turned in unison to look at the manor. Only Knox was able to stay where he was, given his location. "Do you think…"

"No," Orwin denied, emphatically shaking his head. He finally shifted his eyeglasses back into place. "No spirit could cause something like that outside of its immediate confines."

That's not necessarily true, alien hunter. Places are not the only things that can be haunted.

"You're talking about people," I guessed, but not seeing the connection here. "Pearl, Ophelia is definitely attached to the house. We would have felt the shift in our energy had she tried to attach herself to us."

It's not improbable that Ms. Ophelia latched onto something when we exited the manor, Miss Lilura. As we know, nothing is beyond the realm of possibility when dealing with agitated spirits.

We continued to study the house, looking for any type of sign that Ophelia had something to do with what we'd just experienced.

Literally, nothing stood out.

The candles were still lit in the windows, the outside lighting continued to illuminate the enormous building before us, and nothing seemed different than the last time I'd observed the exterior of the manor.

Yet something menacing had shifted in the air.

Oh, what I would do for a spot of warm cream at the moment.

"Isn't there something that we can do from out here?" Knox asked warily, rubbing a hand over his five o'clock shadow. He wasn't used to dealing with this part of the supernatural realm, but I didn't have time to shield him from the inevitable or even make the introductions a bit slower. "I mean, can't we trap whatever is in there? Don't you have some sort of gizmo that can contain it?"

I do like the way this wild beast thinks, dear hexed one.

"Yes, but that's our last resort." I motioned for Orwin and Knox to grab their overnight bags. No matter what happened in the next couple of hours, we were staying inside the manor. We might as well have the essentials. "Orwin, did you bring everything I asked for?"

"Yes."

Orwin practically sighed his reply in resignation, stepping away from Piper as Knox reluctantly opened the back latch of his Land Rover. He was always cautious, but now even more so. We'd just finished a case with a pack of blood-thirsty werewolves, and Knox hadn't hesitated to go up against the entire group singlehandedly.

Your Mr. Emeric doesn't mind dealing with things that he can see and touch. He can use his experience in the military to draw up a strategy to execute, allowing him to utilize his intelligence and physical brawn. Unfortunately, spirits are something that are unpredictable and quite unexplainable to those who don't understand their nature.

"Oh, he believes now," I muttered, turning away so

that I could walk side by side with Piper. Pearl did her disappearing act, but I could sense her presence as we strolled past the other parked cars. "The séance is our only alternative. Ophelia knows what really happened in this place, so we might as well exploit her as a resource. Listen, I saw you reading Eugene's journal when we were inside the great room. You look concerned about something."

No worries, Ms. Lilura. My sweet Piper put all of her notes into that app of hers. I'm in awe of this application, really. Ms. Faye is still the prime suspect, even after the small gem in those old pages were discovered.

"What gem?" I asked, hearing that the men had caught up to us as we finally reached the front entrance of the manor. "What did Eugene write down that you found so interesting?"

"Usually, ghosts who remain behind are here due to unfinished business or their death was so sudden and brutal that they don't believe they are really gone," Piper explained, even though I was already aware of the ins and outs of spirits.

I'd gotten used to her way of sorting information out in her head, which was to usually reiterate details aloud for her own use. It also helped Knox out in situations like these, given his limited awareness of all other things supernatural.

I'd say Mr. Emeric is doing quite well with his crash course of ghouls, goblins, and witches.

I didn't reach for the handle of the door quite yet, as

I wasn't sure if anyone was around the foyer who might be able to hear us once we'd entered the manor. It was best to have these types of conversations in places without prying eyes and listening ears.

We were now all huddled on the doorstep, which was a lot warmer than being out in the wide open of the front cobblestone driveway.

Your warmth wouldn't have anything to do with Mr. Emeric standing by your side, would it, dear hexed one?

"Anyway," Piper continued, her tone suggesting that Pearl needed to leave her fancy notions of romance at the door…no pun intended. "Eugene wrote that Ophelia had died peacefully in her sleep, and that it was expected due to some illness. There was no insinuation that Ophelia had unfinished business, and she certainly didn't die in what one would describe as a horrific manner."

"Why is she still hanging around then?" Knox inquired, shifting his weight to his other boot as he adjusted to entering the domain of a poltergeist. "What does she want?"

That is the question, oh hairy beast.

"That's what we need to find out," I suggested, much to everyone's dismay in a collective group moan. "Seriously? Out of all the creatures we could be dealing with on this case, you're worried about one female entity?"

I didn't wait for them to reply to my question, because I'd meant it figuratively. Unfortunately, sometimes things were beyond my control...like the shrieking scream that perforated the hard wood of the front door. I could literally feel alarm take hold of the group.

Piper, Orwin, and Knox jointly replied a resounding *yes* as I twisted the door handle and we practically all fell onto the marbled tile in a jumbled pile. Faye was holding onto the banister near the staircase landing for dear life with her eyes as wide as a startled doe in the middle of a road in the path of an onrushing vehicle.

"Help me! Please," Faye essentially begged as she lowered herself to a step. "Someone or something tried to push me down the stairs!"

Well, I didn't see this twist coming. I'm definitely going to need that spot of warm cream now, my sweet Piper.

Chapter Nine

"COULD YOU PLEASE tell me what happened one more time?" I asked Faye gently, carefully handing her a hot cup of tea that I'd made in the manor's monstrous kitchen.

I'd seen less equipped kitchens in exclusive clubs and resorts serving hundreds of guests per day. The staff had the benefit of both a walk-in refrigerator and a large freezer behind that. It seemed whomever chose the décor enjoyed the liberal use of stainless steel. Nearly every appliance was of commercial quality and sported a brushed finish. The only large use of wood in the entire kitchen had been a massive butcher-block island where it seemed that the majority of the meals were prepared.

I had used the natural gas twelve-burner stove to heat up the kettle to make Faye her favorite tea. The fan in the overhead vent hood had automatically turned on when the burner ignited. Everyone was on edge, including me as even the fan's whoosh had me startling a smidge off my feet.

Faye was now sitting in the cozy great room in front

of the fireplace on the end of the divan, recovering from her earlier shock. At least we now understood where the harnessed energy had come from when we'd been standing outside in the circular driveway.

"Be careful, please. The tea is very hot."

I must say that spot of warm cream you made for me has taken the edge off of my nerves. They do have a premium quality supplier. Their fresh cream is top notch. That was a very telling incident to see firsthand, wasn't it?

Pearl was talking about the fact that we'd caught sight of Ophelia slowly dissipating from the landing above where we'd found Faye backing down the carpeted steps of the staircase. It was obvious what had taken place, but sometimes the obvious wasn't always as clear as it first appeared.

Knowing the facts of how Ophelia passed away peacefully is what has us questioning ourselves, dear hexed one.

"I had come down to get a glass of water for my nightly medication," Faye replied with a voice that still held a slight tremor of fright. Her blue eyes that had seen many years pass her by slid to the French doors of the great room. "Ever since finding my sister at the bottom of the staircase, I've been very cautious coming down those stairs. I've recently taken to the habit of holding the banister when descending and ascending to my rooms on the upper level. I don't want to think about what would have happened if I hadn't had a firm grip on the railing."

Unfortunately, we know far too well what would have

happened.

"Ms. Ashton, is there anything else we can get you?" Orwin asked, taking a seat next to Faye on the couch. Knox stood next to the roaring fire, his position allowing himself to view the room without worrying about who was coming up behind him. It was a false sense of security, given that an agitated spirit like the one we were currently dealing with could appear out of nowhere. "Knox and I can see you to your room when you're ready to retire for the night."

I remained standing, wondering why Joshua and Izzy hadn't come running when their aunt screamed. Izzy had retired to her room earlier this evening, and Joshua had been in the great room before we'd stepped out of the house to greet our colleagues. It was possible that he'd gone to his own room to watch television, thus disguising Faye's cry for help.

Wilber and Gertrude were probably busy packing in the rear west wing of the manor, so they definitely wouldn't have heard Faye screaming as she was almost pushed to her death. Unless…

Do you suspect that Ms. Ashton is making up the entire story? Well, time will surely tell. Mr. Orwin is now close enough to get a read on this woman's thoughts. Be prepared for anything, dear hexed one.

"What I want is for you to find out if this manor really *is* haunted," Faye declared, her cup clinking against the delicate saucer. She definitely didn't act like a woman who was making a story up as she went along. Besides, we'd seen for ourselves that Ophelia had been on the landing. "I'm ashamed to admit that I didn't believe my sister when she continued to harp on the fact that this place had ghosts. As I mentioned before, my sister could be rather dramatic. She was in the theater during her younger years, and I just figured she'd never outgrown the need for some sort of stage performance."

In this case, that would be the guests of the manor. In case you are wondering, Mr. Cornelia has cleared Ms. Faye of any wrongdoing. Well, other than being a relatively selfish person. She is using her sister's death to get you to stay and help investigate, but I believe she is just afraid of becoming a victim herself.

I had been watching Orwin closely for any signs that he'd been able to pick up on Faye's thoughts. Having Pearl there to communicate his findings helped in this situation, as well as clearing the prime suspect.

Will you look at that? I guess that app isn't all that it's cracked up to be. Perhaps Mr. Cornelia was right in this instance, but I still maintain that technology will be our downfall.

"Ms. Ashton, we don't investigate or dispel hauntings," Piper explained, leaning forward on one of the chairs as she tried to explain our cover story professions. "We just record what happens and then share those tales with our readers."

"But surely you know for certain if there are such things as ghosts," Faye pressed, having relaxed a bit when we didn't come right out and deny her request. "How many manors and estates have you visited? Are there some that you truly believe are haunted?"

Faye laid her worried gaze on each and every one of us, waiting for someone to give her the answer she desired. Surprisingly, it was Knox who stepped forward and steered the conversation to the exact spot I would have if I'd been given the chance.

"Ms. Ashton, were your niece and nephew present here at the manor when your sister passed away?"

Mr. Emeric doesn't mince words, does he?

No, he sure didn't.

"You're not suggesting…" Faye let her voice trail off in horror, taking a healthy gulp of the calming chamomile blend I'd discovered in a wooden box of loose tea leaves in the pantry. I might have added a sprinkle of cantrip magic to aid in that calming measure. Desperation called for desperate measures. "I mean, yes, they were. As a matter of fact, I called them myself to let them know that Florence had been acting very strange lately. Stranger than usual, especially about this haunting business. I never in a million years would have believed…"

"Lou and Piper filled us in on the family argument all of you had this evening." While Knox continued down the same line of questioning, it allowed me to sit back and study Faye's reaction. "Your sister changed her will to where you inherited the estate. That had to make your niece and nephew a tad bit upset."

"Being upset in our family, Mr. Emeric, does not amount to one committing murder," Faye stated matter-of-factly. She was a bit more composed now that she'd sipped half the tea in her cup, but I'm pretty sure it had to do with the sprinkling of magic infused with the essence of passion flower I'd used to help her take the edge off. "Now this ghostly image...well, that's another matter altogether. You've been documenting such cases, and I'd like to hire you to figure out what is really taking place on the Ashton grounds."

No one replied to Faye's request, though she did wait patiently as she sipped the rest of her tea.

I suppose after witnessing Ms. Faye's effect from her beverage, it might behoove me to ask if you did the same to my spot of warm cream.

Like I would ever attempt to use magic on Pearl. It was downright laughable, but I wasn't in the position to give a chuckle at the ludicrous thought. I'd witnessed time and time again what that white feline did in retaliation to Orwin's antics. No, thank you.

I always knew you were wise beyond your years, Miss Lilura.

It was a wonder that Orwin and Piper weren't getting a kick out of this conversation, but it might have had to do with Gertrude's sudden appearance in the doorway.

"What do you mean that you're hiring them to investigate?" Gertrude asked, wringing her hands together in concern. "Isn't it enough that Ms. Ashton has passed on and this estate will never again be used in the manner in which she'd envisioned?"

Oh, dear. Ms. Gertrude appears to be very upset by Ms. Faye's request. You realize, of course, this is the reason one in service should never eavesdrop. It's one of the basic etiquette lessons.

"Gertrude!" Faye exclaimed in dismay, probably at the fact that she wasn't being given the respect she thought she deserved anymore. "These are our guests, and you will—"

"They are your guests, Faye Ashton. Not mine." Gertrude tilted her chin in rejection of Faye's statement. "If you recall, my husband and I handed in our resignations earlier this evening. My darling Florence would have died twice over if she could see the way her family is treating one another now. Despicable. Downright deplorable behavior for cultured, educated people. One would think her children would have learned some measure of decorum just being around our beloved Florence. Her accident not only stole her life, but it took mine and Wilbur's way of life with hers. You're dragging this horrible turn of events out more than needed, and it's a downright shame. Let the woman rest in peace."

I wonder if that speech was self-serving, Miss Lilura. Ms. Gertrude might have taken acting lessons when she was younger, thus fooling us with her reaction to Ophelia's presence on the landing. It's certainly possible, and I don't appreciate being made anyone's fool. I mean, I sent her to the bottom of the list. The least she could have done was reciprocate our good faith.

Gertrude was too far away from where Orwin sat on the couch for him to pick up on her thoughts, and she'd quickly departed in a huff of disappointment before he had a chance to get close to her. She never did say what it was she'd wanted upon her entrance, but I made a mental note to have Orwin run into the couple before they left the premises first thing tomorrow morning.

After all, Gertrude was the one who'd warned us to stay away from room thirteen.

My sweet Piper, I'm afraid Gertrude has been moved up on the list. I'm almost terrified to look at that app. I mean, Ms. Faye has been deleted. Where does that leave us in the suspect pool?

"Ms. Faye, what can you tell us about Ophelia?" I asked, pondering if we'd been right all along.

It would be beneficial to know everything possible about the woman before conducting a séance that could potentially open a portal for her to walk through. I'd never wanted to experience the ramifications of being unprepared, but it was said a spirit could enter one's body if one allowed the door to remain open.

Those pesky devils can be hard to get rid of once they settle into one's corporeal vessel. You did bring cloves with you, right, Mr. Cornelia?

Orwin must have answered Pearl with the correct response, because I heard a sigh of relief mixed in with a bit of satisfaction. It was clear that Knox hadn't followed along with that conversation. After all, he couldn't hear

Pearl and he didn't have Orwin's special ability. His concentration was solely on Faye, waiting for her to supply us with details regarding her ancestor.

"From what I've read, Ophelia was a very docile woman. She was quiet, kind, and what some would say a bit meek. I guess given the time period that wasn't such an uncommon attribute," Faye responded, finishing what was left of her tea. She gently set the empty porcelain cup onto the saucer, allowing both to rest in her lap. "It's my understanding that she loved her husband and their children very much."

Could that be the reason Ms. Ophelia hasn't crossed through the veil? A mother's love is the strongest bond in existence…living or dead.

"From our experience," Piper began to explain as she patted the journals that she'd set on the arm of the chair, "spirits remain behind due to either unfinished business or they just can't accept their passing. I've read in Mr. Eugene's journal that Ophelia died peacefully. There's nothing to suggest that she had unfinished business here or that she wasn't prepared to cross over."

"Eugene and Ophelia had a son and a daughter, whose names were Theodore and Patricia." Faye cast a wary gaze toward the doorway of the foyer. "I'm almost certain that Patricia kept a journal, which would be kept in the family library."

The angst of a young girl knows no bounds, dear hexed one. Ms. Patricia would have used the written word to express her most dire concerns about everyone in her life, especially her parents.

"Let's hope there's more information to find inside her diary." Piper gathered the diaries in her possession and stood, taking a moment to look at her watch. "Lou, should we meet back here a little before midnight?"

I'm still hoping that won't be necessary, dear hexed one. It would be prudent to give my sweet Piper time to discover something in our efforts to help Ophelia cross over into the afterlife.

"Yes, a little before midnight, unless we discover another course of action." That timeframe gave us a little under two hours to figure out if Ophelia was the guilty party to Florence's death. Given the evidence so far, all signs pointed toward the agitated poltergeist roaming the halls of this manor in the dead of night. Orwin should be able to weed out those of the living by twelve o'clock tonight. "Orwin, would you escort Ms. Faye to her bedroom?"

I leaned down to collect the teacup from Faye, grateful to see that her composure remained intact. She'd been through a lot these last few days, and now she'd been attacked by the same spirit that most likely caused her sister's death. I didn't agree with how she handled her niece and nephew, but a bit of leeway was warranted.

"Of course," Orwin responded, standing and holding his hand out for Ms. Faye to take as leverage. "It would be my pleasure."

Who knew the alien hunter had it in him to display proper etiquette? From the way Mr. Cornelia eats with his fingers, one would never have guessed.

"Oh, my nephew could certainly take a few pointers from you," Faye gushed, though her pallor was still a bit off from her previous near-death experience. "I honestly don't know where my sister went wrong. She loved both Izzy and Joshua, and she only wanted what was best for them. They feel slighted over the change in her will, but she didn't exclude them completely. This estate offers many…"

Faye's voice faded away as Orwin escorted her out of the great room and into the foyer. I'd wait for him to return to map out how we were going to get him access to the other suspects this late at night, but it was the only way to clear their names. Afterward, we'd settle in and do what we did best.

Once again, you have a knack of darkening the ambience, Miss Lilura. I think it's best I go check on my sweet Piper now and prepare her for what's to come—a bona fide séance that could mean the end of our little group as we know it.

Chapter Ten

"I'VE GOT TO say, this is truly a first." Knox was still standing next to the blazing fire with his arms crossed in tension. His five o'clock shadow did little to hide his taut jawline. I could only imagine what his reaction would have been had he heard Pearl's ominous declaration. "I know this is a bit macabre, but I think I would have preferred one of the living to have been responsible for Ms. Ashton's death."

I decided to take the teacup and saucer into the kitchen after all was said and done about the séance. It was important to have Knox on board with how things might go down tonight, although not quite in the description that Pearl saw fit to give. I closed the distance, relishing the warmth of the flickering flames after experiencing the chill in the evening air.

"It's better to flat out see evil, isn't it? It makes it simpler to know what's coming in our direction…easier to deal with."

I crossed my arms, much like Knox's position, though not because I was apprehensive. With the tools

Orwin had brought with him in order to conduct the séance, I was quite confident we could pull it off without incident.

Of course, Pearl's stance on the subject had me thinking that maybe nothing could scare me after suffering at the hands of a curse that might very well follow me into the afterlife. She was always spouting that I wasn't optimistic enough, which had me thinking maybe she knew more than she was willing to tell. Regardless of all that, today was the day she got to witness my positivity.

"When Piper and I arrived this morning, we saw Ophelia on the landing," I shared, hoping that my recollection would ease Knox's concern. "She wasn't quite standing there, but more like hovering. I know that all signs point toward Ophelia being responsible for Florence's death, but something isn't right. It could be the fact that someone was using a voodoo doll to control an unearthly spirit, clearly having no conception of what could happen when casting magic without acquiring the proper knowledge."

"You've dealt with spirits before?" Knox asked, the intensity of his gaze heating me in a way the fire never could. I pushed that thought out of my mind…for many reasons. "I thought you said you gave up witchcraft in favor of the academic lifestyle."

"A witch doesn't simply give up her craft," I replied wryly, having wished many times over that were so in my life away from the coven. "There were many spirits I've crossed paths with over the years at the college, the town, and even my apartment building. As for why I walked away to live a normal life, it was because I saw how happy those outside of the coven could be in their daily lives. Those who had no idea of the supernatural world around them were completely happy to just live their lives without all the drama of a ruling coven."

"Does that mean a witch can't find happiness?" Knox asked, curiosity lacing his rich tone.

He continued to study me, but I found his scrutiny to be uncomfortable. I'd always needed to be guarded with what I said about my childhood, so I was instinctively cautious in situations like this.

With Knox?

He seemed to take in so much and store everything he'd seen and heard.

He was also aware I'd grown up inside a coven.

I honestly had no idea why I still felt the need to watch my every word when I was in his presence.

"Of course, that's not the case in reality," I said as flippantly as I could. I guess it couldn't hurt too much to expand my reasoning. "The responsibility of harnessing energy from the earth comes at a price. As with humans, there is good and evil in everyone. Those with good intentions automatically do their best to protect every living creature, even against their own kind when warranted. It's a weight of the responsibility that we carry, and I'd desperately wanted to know what it was like to live life without that heavy burden…especially at the age of eighteen."

Knox had a serious nature much like mine, but I wasn't sure he'd always been like that. He spoke of his family and friends with genuine affection, as well as his past life where he'd all but had the world at his feet. I could easily picture him laughing in the backyard over a smoking grill while hosting a barbeque with a beer in his hand and flipping steaks. It was a shame that he'd had it all taken away in the blink of an eye…by a Lich Queen who had completely succumbed to evil.

"We were the complete opposite at the age of eighteen," Knox shared with a curve of his lips. He rubbed his whiskers as was his tendency when in deep thought. "At eighteen, I didn't have an ounce of responsibility. Not the way you're describing. I wanted to make a difference and save the world. I had no idea what I was getting myself into with the service, but I still don't regret a day I served this country. My training provided me with many intangible benefits that will carry me through even this task."

Knox didn't have to say aloud that he *did* regret taking a day off to go hiking in the woods all those months ago. A harmless adventure had turned his life upside down. It seemed that every time we got closer to finding a cure to these hexes, we were taken down another wayward path to save yet another innocent life.

Maybe this was karma's way of punishing me for walking away from my primary responsibilities at such a young age. Had Pearl been in attendance for this conversation, she would definitely have something to say about my opinion on the subject.

Unfortunately, being in a dire situation like this made it very hard for me to see things optimistically.

"The unsettled vibes you're probably feeling from everyone are in regard to the séance," I shared, not wanting to keep him in the dark longer than necessary. It had nothing to do with the fact that this discussion had turned a bit more personal than I'd wanted it to. "Séances can be tricky if one isn't prepared, but Orwin brought everything we'd need to take the precautions necessary for what we're attempting to achieve tonight."

"You're not tempting fate with that rare sign of optimism, are you?"

Had I not known any better, I would have sworn Knox had been carrying on secret conversations with Pearl. The last thing I needed was for everyone to harp on me even more about my dour attitude over being hexed.

I was allowed to be a bit bitter, right?

I was saved from answering Knox's question when Orwin reappeared from escorting Faye to her room. He seemed to be on a mission, already pushing up his black-rimmed glasses. He went directly to his backpack that he'd lugged inside the manor and set it down next to the coffee table.

"While Piper is looking for the journals of Patricia and Theodore Ashton, I got to thinking about how the estate was previously divided between heirs," Orwin said, sitting down on the couch as he unzipped his backpack. "Faye isn't as bad as her niece and nephew portray her to be. At least, that's not the mentality I'm picking up. The falling out between Faye and Florence had more to do with the fact that Florence received the physical estate, although Faye still maintained a share in the profits...all Ashtons retain their share of the estate's income. Faye just felt slighted by the family tradition back then."

"So, you're saying that the motive isn't about money?" Knox inquired, attempting to decipher Orwin's meaning.

Money isn't a motive? How interesting. You should know that I just left Piper in the comfort of the family library, though the fire has died out with no one to maintain it. Seeing as Gertrude and Wilbur are no longer employed here, I highly doubt that the flames will be rekindled in any of the manor's rooms. You realize that taking money off the motive list in my sweet Piper's app leaves us little to go on...with the exception of Ms. Ophelia. Are we sure that conducting a séance in the presence of a malicious poltergeist who has possibly committed at least one murder is still a good idea, dear hexed one?

"Pearl has a point," Orwin muttered, quickly setting his laptop on his knees and lifting the lid. A sneeze caught him by surprise, telling me that Pearl was close by. "And yes. If I'm right, money isn't the motive."

"What point?" Knox asked warily, tensing those muscles of his again.

Now isn't the time to get sidetracked, Miss Lilura.

Pearl couldn't have missed my glare, but she was thankfully smart enough to refrain from any more comments.

"The point being that conducting a séance does present some challenges." Orwin continued to click away on his keyboard while we waited for the consensus of whatever it was that he was researching. His glasses slid a bit, but he was too engrossed by what was on the screen to care. "Here. I found it. Faye was right, and her thoughts even more so. Izzy and Joshua—"

"Izzy and Joshua what?" A clearly agitated voice came from the foyer. Sure enough, Izzy herself had made an appearance after having left the dinner table in a huff. This allowed me to mark one more suspect off the list, though. I tilted my head so that only Orwin could see my eyes widen with instruction. This was his opportunity to get a lead on her thoughts, and Izzy seemed to catch herself before coming across as unwelcoming. "You must be Ms. Lilura's other colleague. I hope Gertrude saw fit enough to make sure you have everything you need for your overnight stay."

Considering Ms. Izzy pointed out that our stay was only for tonight, I'd say she needed to work on her sincerity. I'm beginning to hanker for another spot of warm cream.

"Izzy, you should know that Gertrude and Wilbur resigned from the manor's employ after you retired to your room," I replied gently, trying to grasp why Izzy was so bitter toward her aunt if what Orwin discovered held even the slightest bit of truth. "Also, your aunt..."

The way I'd spoken softly and hesitantly, breaking off my sentence so that Izzy would become curious was a success. She stepped into the room, slowly closing the distance between us with what appeared to be a worried expression on her face. I believe there was a chance she was being sincere in her concern.

It's hard to take her seriously when I saw Ms. Izzy's duplicity for myself. If you recall, she was kind and seeking solace from you and my sweet Piper one moment...and then in the span of five minutes, she was spouting to her aunt that the only reason she agreed for you to stay in the manor was to buy herself time.

"What about Aunt Faye?" Izzy asked, her suspicious gaze switching in between me and Orwin. "Did she say or do something to cause Gertrude and Wilbur to up and quit? They are like family to us, so something bad must have happened after I left the dinner table. I should have known better than to retire to my room so early."

It didn't escape my notice that Knox was keeping to himself over by the fireplace. I wasn't even sure that Izzy had caught sight of him just yet, but that was probably for the best. Her sole focus was on the conversation at hand, which meant we might finally get some answers.

Oh, our curiosity has already been placated. You see,

Mr. Cornelia has already confirmed that Ms. Faye was telling the truth about the trust funds and the estate. It seems that the estate always falls into the hands of the oldest heir, though every family member has a financial stake in the Ashton holdings.

"Gertrude refused to agree with your brother that the…apparition she saw on the landing was a trick of the light. There was what you might call a slight exchange of words between them that led to Gertrude and Wilbur's resignation," I shared, wondering what being the oldest heir had to do with what Orwin had been researching on his laptop. "You should also know that your aunt almost fell down the same staircase as your mother this evening."

The oldest heir is significant, because Ms. Florence bucked tradition when she decided to change her will to leave the estate to her sister instead of her eldest son…who theoretically would inherit the estate to run as he saw fit.

I could see it was taking a while for Izzy to absorb everything I'd thrown at her, but I was very curious as to why she or her brother would care who ran the estate if every member of the family got their monetary share.

"Is Aunt Faye okay?" Izzy asked, unable to hid the sincere concern in her gaze. She was close enough now that Orwin would be able to hear her unfiltered thoughts, thus discovering Izzy's innocence or guilt. "Where is she?"

You'll be pleased to know that Ms. Izzy had nothing to do with her mother's murder. Mr. Cornelia is picking up quite a lot from Ms. Izzy, including that she has finally noticed Mr. Emeric's presence. Oh, my! That was a racy thought I didn't need to know about, alien hunter.

"I escorted your aunt to her room. She was unharmed, though upset," Orwin replied, having gotten quite good at ignoring Pearl's words of wisdom. He discreetly closed his laptop and slid it inside his backpack. "Lou made her some tea to calm her nerves. I think she'll be okay now. Just a bit shaken, is all."

It was clear to me know that Izzy's gaze kept drifting over to where Knox stood by the fireplace. He was quite tall with a lean muscular build that wasn't covered up by his brown suede jacket he usually wore outdoors. His five o'clock shadow gave him a predatory vibe that any human would chalk up to masculinity. They had no idea just how much of a predator a werewolf could be in their changed form.

That wasn't a hint of jealousy I heard in your tone, was it, dear hexed one?

"Your aunt believes that someone—more like something—pushed her on the landing, Izzy," I explained gently, really wanting to begin this séance so that we could finally seek the answers to this murder mystery. Pearl and her romantic streak were going to be the death of me. "Do you understand what that means?"

Now that Orwin had crossed another suspect off our list, it was time to bring everyone together. The more attendees we had for the séance, the better the draw.

I'm so sorry. I must have missed something important

when I was reading up on tips about courting a werewolf. I also must have heard incorrectly, because I thought you said we should have more attendees for a séance with a murdering ghost on the loose.

Orwin had pretty much given me a double take, as well, but who better to be at the séance than those the spirit wanted to converse with? It made perfect sense, and we did have the tools to minimize the danger.

"Ophelia," Izzy whispered in horror, resting a hand to her chest in fright.

You should know that the same look across Ms. Izzy's face is the exact emotion that is currently causing my beautiful white fur to stand on end. Mr. Cornelia, could I beg you for some assistance in the kitchen? I find myself once again in the need for a spot of warm cream.

"Your aunt wants us to do a bit of investigating into why Ophelia hasn't crossed through the veil, and I just might have an idea," I suggested, hoping to bring Izzy on board with something humans usually saw as fodder for a horror flick. "We want to conduct a séance to find out why Ophelia is haunting the manor."

"A séance?"

"Yes, a séance," I reiterated, confident that we could see this forgathering through in a successful manner. "We'll hold it right here in the great room, far away from the staircase."

I must say, your determination is to be admired, Miss Lilura.

"I'd like to speak with Gertrude before making any

type of rash decision," Izzy replied cautiously, clearly wanting to hear Gertrude's opinion on what she and Joshua witnessed on the landing earlier today. I had no doubt that Gertrude would tell Izzy the truth. "If you'll excuse me, I'll be back shortly."

We all watched together as Izzy left the great room, making her way to the rear west wing of the mansion. Now that Orwin had ruled out two suspects, it was looking more and more like Ophelia was the guilty party. We only had to prove it before finding a turning spell to vanquish her from the manor.

That might be easier said than done, dear hexed one.

"Would someone like to explain to me the behind the scene footage of that conversation?" Knox asked in his usual wry manner. "I really hate not being in on this mindreading business."

He'd closed the distance to stand between me and Orwin, for the first time leaving his post by the fireplace. I'd already explained to him that the rest of the gang didn't necessarily agree with the séance, and it didn't take a genius to figure out that they definitely weren't in favor of adding the Ashton family members to the table.

You see, each of the Ashtons becomes a weak link in our defenses against the spirit we're calling into our presence.

I'd say you're putting that rather mildly, but to each her own, dear hexed one. To each her own.

Chapter Eleven

"JOSHUA IS DOWN the hall in room twenty-four," I whispered, having walked past the room we were staying in. Orwin quietly pointed toward the door that held a specific number, to which I nodded to his silent question. He was making sure that the room in question was the one that housed the voodoo doll. "As soon as you rule out Joshua and Wilbur, I think we should mention that room thirteen isn't being repainted as Ms. Florence indicated before her death."

It was either Pearl or Piper who mentioned that maybe Florence herself had purchased the voodoo doll in an attempt to rid the manor of Ophelia. That scenario was looking more and more likely, but we needed to be sure before we started the séance.

"What's with you and Knox?" Orwin asked quietly as we continued our way down the long hallway.

"Nothing," I was quick to reply, completely blaming Pearl for Orwin even broaching this subject. "Pearl's got some romantic notion in her, right along with that proper etiquette streak that's a mile long. It's annoying as all get out."

Orwin fell silent as we took the final steps that had us stopping in front of Joshua's bedroom door. From the location, I'm sure it was a suite, of sorts. Either case, I wasn't going to stand still and allow Orwin to prod my every private thought. Honestly, I wasn't sure what he would find, and I honestly didn't want to know.

The sole focus of my life was finding a cure to this hex.

I couldn't have anything else interfere, especially whatever fancy notion might pop into Pearl's tiny little head.

Orwin pushed up his black-rimmed glasses and parted his lips to comment, but I quickly held up a hand for him to stop before he got ahead of himself.

"Not one word if you still want me to get you that new Alienware laptop," I warned, giving him a sideways glare.

"I wasn't going to say a thing."

Orwin motioned with his hand that I should take the initiative and knock on Joshua's door. Since my arm was already raised, I simply connected my knuckles to the hard surface. This shouldn't take long. The goal was for Joshua to answer allowing Orwin to get a read on his thoughts, basically clearing the way for us to have just one suspect left—Ophelia.

That wasn't to say that some other staff member couldn't have done the horrific deed, being sent home when Faye had dismissed most of the staff. After all, the roster of employees Orwin had pulled from the estate's software was quite extensive, including a full list of groundskeepers.

But something told me that the murderer was close by, thus resulting in those specific people...and the one spirit...currently inhabiting this manor.

Piper was the one who'd gone exploring earlier today while I'd stayed in the room to construct the list of materials we'd need from the RV. Knox was currently retrieving those items from the Land Rover, though he didn't seem too happy that we'd left him to his own resources.

"Who would have thought that Knox would be scared of an itty-bitty ghost," Orwin commented with a small smirk of his face. The two men got along quite well, most likely because their talents were completely different from one another. They were polar opposites. That didn't mean one wouldn't goad the other when it was right there for the taking. "Don't you think another word, Lou. I know I'd come out on the losing end in comparison to that man. Whatever strain of lycanthropy Ammeline cursed him with made him stronger and larger than the average werewolf."

I didn't miss Orwin's reference to the old saying 'smarter than the average bear'.

"Not nice," I whispered in return right before I heard the faint sounds of footsteps coming closer to the door. It wasn't that I needed to defend Knox. Not in the least. For some reason, it was instinctive for all my team members. Once again, I wasn't going to waste time ruminating over something that was irrelevant to our immediate future. "Mr. Ashton, we're sorry to disturb you. This is my colleague, Orwin Cornelia."

"Did you guys feel that earthquake?" Joshua asked, having come to the conclusion that was why we were paying him a visit at eleven o'clock at night. It didn't surprise me to find that his cell phone was still in his hand, which he'd moved to his left in order to greet Orwin. The two men shook hands, and I tried not to continuously study Orwin's expressions to see what his reaction was to reading Joshua's thoughts. "It was just a slight tremor, but I've only ever experienced them on the West Coast."

It was good to know that we weren't the only ones who had felt the jolt of energy. There was no doubt in my mind that it had come from Ophelia's attempt to push Faye down the stairs. It took a lot of energy for a spirit to do something like that, especially twice in the span of three days.

I quickly glanced at Orwin, but it seemed as if he were still compiling his opinion.

"Actually, we came to tell you about some new developments." I paused briefly when I saw movement out of my peripheral vision, but the hallway was empty. "Your aunt almost fell down the stairs this evening, and she doesn't believe she took a misstep. She's okay physically, but she's really shook up."

I gave Joshua time for my words to sink in, hoping that Ophelia hadn't gathered enough energy to make another appearance. We needed a bit more time to convince Joshua that a séance was a good idea, but who knew what his reaction would be at seeing Ophelia float down the hallway.

"Aunt Faye always talked about how dramatic my mother could be, but it's nothing compared to the acting abilities that woman has. Don't let her fool you."

Joshua went to close his bedroom door when Orwin took me by surprise and lodged his black boot just inside the doorframe. He'd done so in time to stop the door from being slammed shut in our faces.

"You're wrong about the reason your mother took your name out of contention to run the estate," Orwin stated matter-of-factly. My first instinct was to slap him upside the back of his head. What was he thinking, exposing himself like that to a human? "Your mother broke the tradition of leaving the Ashton family estate to the oldest heir because she realized that your aunt had nothing else…and it was with the sole stipulation that you inherit the position as head of the estate upon Faye's passing. I know this to be true, because I hacked into the estate lawyer's firm to read the will in its entirety. On Monday, you'll receive the letter that your mother meant only for you. You'll understand her decision better then, and maybe your family can make amends with one another before any more damage is done."

Orwin wasn't one to get too philosophical. He left that type of sentiment to Pearl, but he'd done a fine job in getting Joshua to look at his situation a bit differently and without anger. I was truly impressed with the way he'd handled this situation, though it would have been nice to have been let in on what he'd discovered with those hacking skills of his.

Usually, Pearl was pretty good at communicating things between us when Orwin couldn't talk freely. She'd gone in search of Piper, though, and no doubt would attempt to wrangle another spot of warm cream before joining in on the séance.

"Izzy asked you to hack into our estate lawyer's computer system?" Joshua asked skeptically, leaning a forearm against the open door. He pointed his phone in the direction of Izzy's room. "My sister…the one who abides by all the rules?"

I honestly hadn't thought of Izzy as a woman who followed all the rules and regulations, but I might have cast judgements a bit early, especially given the circumstances. The one thing I was really good at was casting magic and knowing when Orwin was comfortable around someone. He'd relaxed his stance and moved his boot out of the way to allow Joshua the option of listening to us further or continuing to slam the door in our faces.

"Yes, in a roundabout way," I hedged, not wanting the siblings to compare notes before we'd solved the murder mystery and vacated the estate. "You see, Faye believes it was Ophelia who tried to push her down the stairs. She also thinks that your mother's death might not have been an accident, after all, and has asked us to look into the matter. We aren't the police, of course. Our methods are a bit more...untraditional."

"What's that mean?" Joshua asked bluntly, his gaze bouncing off me and Orwin.

Once again, I caught something move in my peripheral vision. It was a massive relief to see Piper standing and waiting for us at the end of the hallway, gesturing for us to go downstairs. I nodded my understanding, unable to handhold Joshua anymore.

"Izzy is speaking to Gertrude about what the two of you saw on the landing of the staircase," I shared, right as Orwin sneezed. Pearl had made an appearance of sorts, and I braced myself for any news that might change the course we'd mapped out. "Joshua, what did you see? You kept saying at dinner that it could have easily been a trick of the light. If you have any doubts, wouldn't you want to know if your mother's death wasn't an accident?"

Very well stated, dear hexed one. I have no doubt that Mr. Joshua will be joining us for the séance. You'll be pleased to know that I've fortified myself with a spot of warm cream, and can now concentrate on the task at hand.

"Everyone is gathering in the great room," Orwin

explained, pulling a tissue out of the front pocket of his khakis. He discreetly wiped his nose before continuing. "We're conducting a séance to see if we can speak with Ophelia's spirit."

"A séance?" The disbelief in Joshua's tone was more than evident, and I tried not to take it too personally. It was very hard for humans to believe in the supernatural, but his reaction also told me that he wasn't the one who'd been dabbling in voodoo. "You can't possibly be serious. What's next? A Ouija board? That is the most ridiculous—"

"Mr. Ashton, I explained that our methods were a bit unorthodox," I said, cutting off what was sure to be a long explanation as to why such things didn't work. "Your aunt and sister are on board with the idea. Gertrude and Wilbur will be joining us, and we'd like you to do the same. The more energy we are able to produce, the better chance we stand of communicating with Ophelia."

Let's just hope that we can contain that energy, Miss Lilura. From the effects of Ophelia's previous appearance, I'd say she is quite strong. Odd, really, given the fact that Piper found something very interesting in Patricia's diary.

I motioned for Orwin to begin walking back the way we'd come, fishing out my room key in case Joshua remained in the doorway to watch us leave. He still stood inside the doorframe with a dubious expression on his face. He was such a nonbeliever of the supernatural—

even after having seen a spirit with his own eyes—that I wasn't sure we could convince him to join us at the séance.

"We'll be downstairs, Mr. Ashton," I said with a finality that ended the discussion.

Bravo, Miss Lilura. Now, what exactly do you plan to do once you retrieve the voodoo doll?

Now that we had close to all the players in the great room, I planned to keep the momentum moving along. With Orwin on board, we were unraveling information at a rapid rate.

I suppose that's a good thing with Ophelia needing to recharge before attempting to take someone's life again.

It didn't take long for Orwin and I to reach room thirteen. I made it seem as if the key I held in my hand was the one to actually go to this specific keyhole, all the while using my mind to shift the lock mechanism. I didn't even look back to see if Joshua was still watching us. The second I heard the lock unfasten, I turned the handle and walked inside the room without hesitation.

Well, I'm not quite sure what to think of this new turn of events.

Neither was I.

The room was completely furnished, and there wasn't a voodoo doll in sight.

"I thought you said that this room was empty and that it was basically a shrine for a voodoo doll," Orwin muttered, walking past the armoire to where a beautiful four poster bed had been pushed up against the far wall.

"Are you sure we're in the right room?"

Hoping beyond hope that I'd opened the wrong door, I backtracked a few steps to get a glimpse at the golden brass numbers. Once again, and far too many times to count over these last few months, my hope evaporated into thin air.

We were definitely standing in room thirteen.

"That's odd." Joshua must have decided to join us downstairs, because he'd appeared in the doorway. I turned in time to see him glancing around the room with curiosity. "Mother told us that this room was being renovated."

Dear hexed one, I have a feeling that Ms. Florence might have known more about her ghost problem than we originally thought. It's my guess that this room was always furnished…even when we were inside of it earlier today.

"Ophelia wanted us to see what the room was like years ago," I murmured, still trying to piece together what had transpired earlier today. Everything surrounding us had seemed so real. Thinking back, we hadn't touched anything for fear of disturbing the energy without having a way to channel it. Had we even brushed a finger over the voodoo doll, chances are the illusion would have dissipated into a misty ripple, eventually allowing us to see what was truly in front of us. "Why would she show us that particular memory from her past?"

I presume it's finally time to ask Ms. Ophelia ourselves. Are you ready to host your first séance, dear hexed one?

Chapter Twelve

"ARE YOU SURE there was nothing in Ophelia's diary about visiting someone who practiced voodoo, maybe in New Orleans, or dabbling in it herself?" I asked Piper, though I made sure no one could overhear our conversation. "Ophelia is stronger than we originally thought. What if there's a chance she is more than just a mere ghost? Have you ever heard of a wraith or a specter inhabiting an occupied dwelling before? Even then, I've never heard of either one having spell casting capability. Think about it, though. Ophelia made two witches and a familiar believe they saw something that wasn't there. A phantasm of that strength takes powerful magical ability. We aren't dealing with your average everyday novice ghost."

That's an understatement, Miss Lilura. You should know that Mr. Emeric seems to have lost a bit of color underneath that five o'clock shadow of his. I daresay the man nor the wolf within him likes the thought of trying to prevent a poltergeist from taking another life.

While Orwin and I had been upstairs attempting to

convince Joshua to join in on the séance, Knox had taken the items he'd retrieved from the Land Rover and set them on a table in the middle of the great room. Afterward, we'd spent the last half an hour rearranging the furniture and stowing the knickknacks to ensure the upcoming event wasn't hindered by inanimate objects flying about.

As for Piper, she'd found Patricia's personal diary in the family library.

All resource and determination, that one.

Once she'd had it in hand, she'd returned to the great room and went about lighting candles and setting the proper ambiance. She also burned the appropriate herbs in a plain porcelain dish to cleanse the room of anything that could prevent Ophelia from communicating with us, mindful not to use any sage to block the one entity we needed to speak with.

We had one shot at this, because this agitated spirit was smart enough not to get caught out in the open and make herself vulnerable twice.

I'm not so sure that Ms. Ophelia will fall for our trap in the first place, Miss Lilura. She is no one's fool.

"If Ophelia is as smart as we think, she already knows that this séance is a risk for all of us," Orwin muttered, backing up Pearl's supposition. He carefully lifted the lid on a thousand-year-old white oak box that we'd retrieved from a shaman before we'd begun this entire journey to find a cure. As a matter of fact, we'd accumulated quite a lot of unique and extraordinary items to combat the innumerable evils drifting through the supernatural realm. White oak, with the proper runes carved in the lid of the box, could snare nearly any non-corporeal being. "We're as prepared as we're ever going to be."

Shall we get this séance started then, dear colleagues?

Not yet, but soon.

I wanted a little more time to gather some intimate details on Ophelia. One never knew what could come in handy during communicating with the dead.

Faye, Izzy, and Joshua were all sitting on the couch, all but ignoring one another. Gertrude and Wilbur were on the loveseat across from them, sitting stiff as boards. Orwin had stood next to Wilbur for less than twenty seconds before signing to us that the man did not kill his employer. Orwin divulged to us a bit later that Wilbur actually couldn't wait to leave this manor and the people inside of it, because he was totally convinced that they were all completely insane.

Mr. Wilbur wouldn't technically be too far off the mark.

"I skimmed through the pages, but I didn't find any mention of a voodoo doll," Piper responded distractedly, turning another page. She'd parked herself in the overstuffed chair to get through as much of Patricia's diary as she could before we began the main event. "I'm reading about the passing of her mother now, which happened just as Eugene had described in his journal.

What I do find interesting was Patricia's overall opinion of her father. Apparently, he was quite obsessed with maintaining the Ashton estate and the fortune that came with it. He was a workaholic, barely spending any time with the family. The only one who could get him to leave his office was Ophelia."

A discreet cough came from one of the Ashtons.

That would be Ms. Faye, using the proper etiquette to gain someone's attention.

"Do we really need to have so many candles burning in here?" Faye inquired, her fixed gaze remaining on Knox as he began closing the curtains at my request. "The fire isn't enough?"

I'm rethinking her decorum. Clearly, she missed a class or two regarding rudeness.

"Fire is an element of the earth, and therefore is considered a beacon for those spirits on the other side," I explained, figuring this brief introduction to séances would allow Piper the time needed to find anything else hidden within Patricia's diary. "The more flames we have calling out to Ophelia, the better."

"Isn't she already here?" Joshua asked impatiently, clearly annoyed with himself that he'd caved under the pressure of curiosity and decided to join the group. "I mean, Aunt Faye insists that Ophelia tried to push her down the stairs. Isn't that why we're here? To carry on this charade and get our minds off the fact that Mother changed her will?"

I'm throwing this out there with every good intention,

but wouldn't it be prudent for the Ashtons to come to some kind of truce? You, of all witches, understand the importance of a calm atmosphere. "Your mother and I—" Faye was cut off from explaining what had taken place between her and Florence before the matriarch's death.

"I know, I know. The two of you came to some sort of agreement and made peace with one another," Joshua said, waving a hand in disgust. They all began carrying on as if there weren't strangers in attendance. "Neither one of you seemed to care that you were throwing away my entire inheritance."

"Don't you mean *our* inheritance?" Izzy said, leaning back against the cushion and crossing her arms in a defensive manner. One wouldn't guess that she was in her forties. "You promised me that we would run the estate together." "Well, thanks to Mother and Aunt Faye, neither one of us is going to be running the estate until we're old and penniless." Joshua switched his frustration from his family to me. "Is this farce really necessary?"

It was only a matter of time before one of the Ashtons turned their frustration toward us, dear hexed one. I hope you are prepared to lay the groundwork for that calm atmosphere we were just discussing.

I took a brief moment to center myself, fully prepared to do what needed to be done. There was no use trying to cast a spell to bring a family like this together, because then it really wasn't of their own free will. Certain arcane charm enchantments could keep them from each other's throats, but they all held animosity in their hearts for one another. That hostility weakened the spell's effect and duration.

There are times I don't think I give you enough credit, dear hexed one.

Orwin covered up his laugh with a sneeze, which was probably his repayment to karma for getting humor out of Pearl's witty comment. Piper was the smart one. She continued to leverage this time by delving deeper into Patricia's diary. There had to be something about the voodoo doll inside one of those journals.

"Mr. Ashton, what we do isn't a farce," I replied, sensing that Knox had taken up his position next to the hearth. The room was quite warm, given the many sources of heat, but that was exactly what we needed to happen in order to lure Ophelia out from hiding. She hadn't shown herself once since her attempt to push Faye down the stairs. "Your mother didn't believe our ability to seek out spirits was a farce, either."

Joshua compressed his lips and feigned fixing the sleeve of his buttoned-down dress shirt. He hadn't bothered putting back on his suit jacket or tie, comfortable in being more casual with his folded cuffs.

"I'm going to give you our thoughts on what's been happening here, conduct the séance to reach Ophelia, and finally clear up what reason she would have to murder one of her descendants. After we've completed each of those tasks, the three of you are free to continue

arguing over material wealth until your hearts' content."
I'd make sure they understood the importance of a calm
atmosphere after my speech, but I was hoping my words
did the job for me. "The Ashton family tradition has
been carried out over the centuries—the oldest child of
the following generation is the one who inherits the
control over business components of the estate."

"You're not telling us anything we don't know, Miss
Lilura," Faye practically scolded me, picking off some
imaginary lint from her black dress.

"Is there a reason you didn't tell your nephew about
the letter his mother left him?" I asked, getting to the
heart of the matter. It was coming up on midnight. The
witching hour only lasted until one. "I'm guessing you
didn't mention it because you wanted him to understand
your sister's reasoning. You want the admiration and
respect of Izzy and Justin, but you're afraid they won't
see past your previous mistakes the way Ms. Florence
came to during those six months you stayed here with
her."

Faye was doing her best not to make eye contact with
Izzy and Joshua. I could tell Izzy was a bit lost, so I
caught her up to speed hoping that the truth didn't come
out.

"Izzy, your mother left both of you letters to be given
to you during the reading of the will." While I continued
to try mending fences, Orwin finished setting up the
room. "In those letters are the reasons for her choices,

and also the explanation of how the stipulation on her new will shall be carried out upon Faye's death."

Orwin came up behind me and whispered a detail that put things in a new perspective. Faye's inner fears had risen to the surface, allowing him to catch her most vulnerable thoughts.

That is quite interesting, and actually explains Ms. Faye's behavior. I guess I shouldn't be so harsh to judge one's decorum without fully knowing all the facts.

"You see," I said, directing my next statement toward Izzy and Joshua. "Your aunt wasn't fully convinced that your mother's death was an accident. The reason Ms. Faye asked you to leave for the weekend and return on Monday was for fear that one of you might actually try to take her life...thus returning the estate back into Joshua's hands."

"How did you—" Faye's dismay was cut off by her niece.

"Wait a second," Izzy exclaimed, straightening from her slouching position and staring at her aunt in horror. "You thought we'd try and kill you? How could you think we would do something like that? Do you truly believe we're that terrible of human beings?"

Well, isn't this an unexpected turn of events? I'm beginning to feel sorry for Ms. Izzy. Her horrified reaction says it all.

"You have to understand that I was just looking out for myself," Faye defensively added, resting a hand against her chest. "I knew how the two of you would react, and I...well, I might have overreacted after all that's happened."

Alien hunter, I hope you know that all of our bantering is in good faith.

Pearl was attempting to ease Orwin's mind about all the pranks they'd pulled on one another, reassuring him that she would never truly follow through on her teasing threat to send messages to beings in outer space all but saying that he was a prime individual ready to be abducted.

"Hey, I never believed that," Orwin muttered in my ear as he walked behind me to join Knox near the hearth.

Don't let him fool you, Miss Lilura. He believed every word. I had him going there for quite a while, but after witnessing this debacle of a family...I thought it was time to clear the air.

"Wow." Joshua ran a hand over his face in disbelief. "What did we ever do to you that you would think we were capable of such an evil act?"

"There have been a lot of strange things happening in this house that I couldn't explain, and I didn't believe your mother when she tried to tell me this place was haunted by spirits," Faye explained, hesitantly glancing toward the French doors that we'd let remain open. "I figured those strange noises and haunting moans in the middle of the night were staged to scare us. The only thing that made sense to me was that she'd told one of you about the will, and that you were trying to drive me out of this place with some crazy ghost story."

"Ms. Faye is right about the strange noises and haunting moans," Gertrude fessed up, finally joining in on the conversation. She snuck a glance toward Wilbur, who reluctantly nodded a confirmation. "It took me a while to figure out it was Ophelia, just as Ms. Florence said. She calls for her husband almost every night."

"Did you really feel Ophelia push you, Aunt Faye?" Izzy asked quietly, tentatively reaching out to hold her aunt's hand. Faye's astonishment at such a comforting gesture was evident. "I'm so sorry…for everything."

I'm beginning to understand why you taught psychology, dear hexed one. Very well done. I couldn't have done better myself.

Unfortunately, I wasn't able to use what I knew on the subject on a troubled spirit. Speaking of that particular entity, there was a minor shift in the air. I couldn't put my finger on the change, but a quick glance over my shoulder revealed that the others sensed it, as well.

"Aunt Faye, I'm sure after we read Mom's letters that we'll understand her decision better," Joshua relented, taking Izzy's hand when she reached out with her free one. "I—"

The flames of the candles began to flicker the moment Joshua began speaking, almost as if they were being caressed by a gentle breeze. By the time he was done, the air had begun to circulate in what could only he called a violent rage.

Every single candle was extinguished, the journals Piper had balancing on the arm of the chair fell to the floor, and the French doors slammed shut with a deafening crash.

It appears that Ophelia has something to tell us, Miss Lilura. We best not keep her waiting.

Chapter Thirteen

"EVERYONE, PLEASE REMAIN calm," I recommended as gently and serenely as I could. It was quite hard to do when my heart was racing double what it normally beat in any given minute. "Ophelia will have trouble communicating to us what she wants without opening up some sort of portal to the other side. It's more than apparent that she has something on her mind."

You might be understating Ophelia's desire just a tad bit, dear hexed one. That was some entrance.

Truthfully, I was surprised that no one had all but accused us of scamming them with special effects. Their silence and acquiesce told me they'd experienced enough supernatural elements that they might actually be true believers now.

It does make our job a bit easier, doesn't it? Now, shall we relight those candles?

"What does she want?" Izzy cried out, her hair not as smooth as what it had been earlier. As a matter of fact, the collective group of the Ashton clan's pallor resembled ghosts themselves. "Why is she doing this?"

"That is what we're going to try to find out," I reassured her, nodding to each and every one of them so that they had as much confidence in my answer as I did. "Please, take a seat on the floor around the coffee table while we finish getting things ready."

Orwin pushed up his glasses as he began lighting the candles once more. Pearl must be keeping her distance from him to prevent the others from asking why his allergies had suddenly become so bad.

I witnessed the alien hunter taking his allergy medication before everyone gathered round. Upon more thought, it is quite funny that he believed the little green men would be interesting in abducting him for research purposes. I'm fairly certain a higher species would choose a specimen with higher quality DNA.

Meanwhile, Knox readjusted each of the curtains back into position. The intense frown on his face told me what he'd already conveyed—he'd rather deal with other monsters, vampires, and zombies than he would a spirit that had the ability to remain invisible.

"Lou," Piper called out, waving her hand at me to come closer. "Did you know that Eugene Ruthsford Ashton died falling off the very same roof that is currently over our heads?"

Ohhhh, another twist. These mysteries are such good cardio workouts, aren't they?

"That is correct," Faye replied, carefully positioning herself on one of the long sides of the oval coffee table so that her dress remained in place. Izzy and Joshua joined her, all nodding their agreement on family history. "From the stories, our Eugene suffered terribly for days before he perished with Patricia by his side."

"Aren't those the spirits who usually hang around to haunt a place like this?" Wilbur asked in his aged voice. He was pretty limber for his years on this earth, so it wasn't surprising to find him helping Gertrude lower herself to the ground. "I heard you mention that earlier."

"Yes, that's right," I responded, wondering what else had occurred at Eugene's bedside before his death. "Piper, what else does Patricia write in her diary about that dark time?"

Orwin took a seat next to Gertrude, pushing up his glasses and patting her hand in reassurance. I tilted my head in gesture toward Knox in an attempt to get him to join, but he was having none of that.

Now, this ought to be fun.

"Stop that," I muttered, figuring I was going to have enough trouble to get Knox to sit down on the floor with the others as it was. "Go help Piper or something."

Why? My sweet Piper has that fancy app of hers. Look, she's typing in the new information now. I thought we'd come to the conclusion that technology isn't all that it's cracked up to be. Apparently, I was the only one of that opinion.

I could see from Piper's expression that she was reassuring her familiar that she could never be replaced, even by technology. It was so rare that Pearl ever doubted herself, it made me wonder if Ophelia wasn't trying to attempt to talk to us in a different manner altogether.

I mean, possession by an agitated spirit wasn't unheard of in our world.

Have you gone mad, dear hexed one? I've been on the face of this earth for over two thousand years. Trust me when I say that I am well warded in the possession department from a poltergeist. Technology is another story altogether. Who knows what artificial intelligence is capable of when we don't understand its limitations?

I'm sure Pearl could have gone on and on about the unknown dangers of technology, but that was for another time. Right now, we had one really upset spirit to deal with before anyone else was hurt or worse…killed.

Orwin was instructing those at the coffee table what would happen in the coming moments, such as how we would all hold hands in unity as we called upon Ophelia to communicate with us. It was vital that the chain of hands not be broken or else our tenuous connection to the afterlife would be severed as well.

"Knox, please come join us," I urged once I made my way over to where he was standing next to the hearth. The golden hue of his eyes was practically as bright as the flickering flames behind him, and his intense gaze was completely focused on the French doors that were currently still closed. "The more energy we have at the table, the easier it will be to communicate with Ophelia."

It appears that Mr. Emeric's stubborn streak might be

hampering our efforts, Miss Lilura.

"Do you hear that?" Knox asked, narrowing his stare when he tilted his head slightly.

He wasn't referring to Pearl's opinion, but instead some sound he was picking up from elsewhere else in the mansion. A werewolf's senses were heightened beyond imagination.

Knox could hear and recognize a specific howl from over five miles away. His sense of smell could distinguish one sample of blood from another at twenty paces, and he could detect the presence of another supernatural being by their lack of human pheromones.

The most powerful sense available to a werewolf besides smell was his visual acuity. He could read a book from across the road at night in little to no moonlight. Nothing much was going to escape his attention.

"I don't hear anything," I replied quietly, not wanting to alarm the others. "Knox, please come join us."

"I've been catching sounds of a...well, a screech." Knox shook his head slightly when he couldn't distinguish what the high-pitched squeal was or where it was coming from. "I thought it was coming from the plumbing or electrical equipment of the manor, but now I'm not so sure."

I'm not so sure you'll be able to convince Mr. Emeric to join us, dear hexed one. We're wasting precious time, and you know how important the witching hour is to this endeavor.

"I realize that Ammeline threw you into a life you

never believed existed before, and I haven't given you enough credit for adjusting as fast as you have this past year." I've always been a little guarded, but most witches were when it came to the supernatural realm. After being hexed, my need to protect myself became even more imperative. I could only imagine what it was like for Knox to be on the receiving end of something he didn't believe in. "It's terrifying, mind-numbing, and so farfetched that you think you're losing your sanity. I'm right there with you, and I question every day if we'll ever find a cure to these curses. But this family has no idea that the supernatural walks beside them and that it was responsible for Florence's death. We might be able to offer them some small measure of closure, Knox."

You rendered me speechless, dear hexed one. Well done. Well done.

I barely refrained from rolling my eyes at Pearl's praise. She was always telling me to be more open, to share my feelings, and to allow myself to enjoy the fleeting moments of happiness that slipped through this hex of mine.

That was easier said than done.

"Fine." Knox compressed his lips before pointing a finger toward my chest. "If you start speaking in tongues or if that thing takes over your body…all bets are off."

My face literally hurt as I did my best to prevent my smile from spreading at his defensive stance against the unknown. I pursed my lips and nodded solemnly in agreement to whatever it was he thought he could do if those things did happen…which technically weren't out of the question. I could only imagine what it would be like if Knox turned while sitting at the table with our guests immediately after I started speaking with a disembodied voice.

Fortunately for us, we know how to avoid such mistakes. I double-checked the alien hunter's work on the runes inside the lid of the white oak box that was made for exactly these kinds of circumstances, and I daresay I'm somewhat impressed with his precision in such matters.

"It looks as if we're ready," I said quietly, nodding toward Piper to join us. She carried the journals with her and kneeled next to Knox on the opposite end, setting the intimate details of the Ashton family next to her on the large area rug. The two of them were both on their knees facing the French doors. I didn't care for having my back toward any entrance or exit, either, but this certainly wasn't normal circumstances. "Everyone hold hands, please. Whatever happens, please do not break the circle. Do not let go."

I'm right next to you, dear hexed one.

I, too, settled on my knees, reaching for Orwin's hand to my left. I had done the same to Joshua, who had a similar expression to Knox in that he'd rather be anywhere else but here. It didn't surprise me to find that Joshua's palm was cold in his apprehension. Quite the contrast to mine, given that I was confident this séance was our only ticket to the truth.

Unable to help myself, I gave Knox a wink of encouragement before closing my eyes and inviting the surrounding energy to enter my body. Almost in unison, I could hear everyone's breath hitch. A group tended to follow their leader, so I began to even out my inhalations and exhalations to establish composure amongst the participants.

What a touching gesture you just gave—

I shifted, knowing for a fact that Pearl was to my right from the direction of her English-accented voice.

Right, right. You were just reassuring Mr. Emeric, that's all. I shouldn't be so presumptuous.

The sarcasm was practically dripping from Pearl's words, and I wasn't happy that Orwin and Piper could hear our exchange. We were all in this together, and I was just trying to get Knox comfortable with the supernatural realm.

Now wasn't the time to be having this conversation anyway, so I did my best to block everything out but the rhythmic tick of the grandfather clock in the corner of the room. The seconds slowly melded with my heartbeat until I was prepared for what came next.

Shall we begin, dear hexed one?

Chapter Fourteen

"OPHELIA ROSALYN ASHTON, we call upon you to join us in whatever form you can."

The sound of my own voice was like a cannon being shot inside the great room. Of course, it was nothing like the dramatic deep chime when the grandfather clock had struck twelve times to signify that it was the witching hour.

Oh, how exciting is this?

One minute, Pearl was voicing her concern about the consequences of such a séance, and now she was enjoying herself?

Now that I've double-checked Mr. Cornelia's fail safe, I certainly am. This is magic at its best, dear hexed one. Oh, and the additional spot of warm cream might have eased my concern, as well.

"Ophelia Rosalyn Ashton, we call upon you to join us at this table," I repeated, holding firmly to those hands in my grasp. "Show us a sign you are with us."

Yes, please. Communicate with us, dear Ophelia.

I slowly lifted my lashes to find that most everyone was focused on the French doors. They could concentrate all they wanted on the double entrance, but I was more concerned with the flickering flames of the candles. Orwin and Piper were studying the burning wicks, as well, looking for telltale signs that we were no longer alone. Knox, on the other hand, was staring at me rather intensely.

Isn't he such a gentleman? Mr. Emeric is making sure that you're okay, dear hexed one. He gets super special bonus points.

"Ophelia, I know you wish to communicate with your family," I continued, slowly moving my gaze about the room for any indication that the agitated spirit was near. "They are gathered here to hear your message. Please let us know that you're with us."

The mere flicker of the flame on the mantle of the hearth gave me hope that Ophelia was about to answer our request, in spite of Pearl's commentary.

I'm helping, in case you hadn't noticed, dear hexed one. From Ms. Ophelia's previous visits, a mere familiar wouldn't prevent her from materializing.

"You've waited a long time to convey your message, Ophelia."

That's an understatement, but I'm sure she'll understand your efforts, Miss Lilura.

I paused my plea for a moment, allowing the spirit to garner the energy it would take materialize. Some spirits only communicated through noises, Ouija boards, and intermediates like mediums. We knew for a fact that Ophelia had utilized those years she'd been earthbound to perfect her ability to cross over with a certain amount of force.

"Your family is gathered around in the very room you spent time with your husband and children, Ophelia. They'd like the opportunity to hear what you have to say."

I'm not so sure about that, given the fact that they are mere seconds away from panicking.

The collective gasps that came from those surrounding the coffee table wasn't surprising, especially given that Ophelia didn't gradually materialize in front of us. No, she chose to enter the room with a bang—specifically by blowing the doors wide open.

Those mere flickers of the candle flames had just been Ophelia having a bit of fun. She's finally here…

"Do not break the circle," I called out, holding tight to Joshua's hand before he could break the circle. I didn't have to worry about Orwin, who was currently sniffling up a storm due to his allergies. "Maintain contact at all times!"

"Eugene…"

Those collective gasps I'd mentioned? Well, I'm pretty sure Izzy screamed and Faye came close to fainting at the sight of Ophelia hovering in the doorway. I figure the only reason they continued to hold hands was that their grips were like vises.

I'm monitoring their responses, dear hexed one. Please concentrate on our guest so that we don't somehow end up slipping off to the other side of the veil. I'm certainly not ready to leave just yet.

Ophelia's ethereal presence wasn't calm, as were most visitors from the other side. The frantic way she kept looking around the room was rather unsettling. The wisps of her form gracefully flowed in each direction she turned, still calling out her husband's name.

"Ophelia, why has your spirit remained here with us on this plane?" I asked, unable to pinpoint why Ophelia seemed so agitated instead of angry. She'd pushed Florence to her death before attempting the same to Faye. I had fully expected fury and rage to be seeping from the apparition in front of us. "What is it that is keeping you from crossing over?"

"Eugene…"

Ophelia's energy was filled with such angst, her sorrow was like tidal waves breaking on the rocks.

We might have a problem, dear hexed one. Ms. Faye is practically bubbling over with grief, as are Ms. Izzy and Mr. Joshua.

"Why did you kill my sister?" Faye asked, crying out in a way that had me worried she'd break our bond. The older woman was shaking with fear, but it was Ophelia's sorrow that had Faye reacting without thinking. "Why would you do that?"

"Eugene…"

Call for Mr. Eugene. It's clear that Ms. Ophelia will not answer anyone until she speaks with her husband. It's only a matter of time before this séance becomes too much for the Ashtons. Do it now, dear hexed one.

"Eugene Ruthsford Ashton, we call on you through the veil. We ask that you cross over and speak with your wife," I requested, grateful that Pearl was able to read the situation clearly while I was able to focus on the white oak box Orwin had set up in case things went south. "Eugene Ruthsford Ashton, we call on you through the—"

The rage I'd expected to experience when Ophelia made her presence known suddenly entered the room, but the penetrating emotion didn't emanate from her…

I'm ashamed to admit it, but we've been wrong this entire time. If this situation and Mr. Eugene cannot be controlled, there is only one thing left to do…

You see, Eugene Ruthsford Ashton didn't come through the veil. He'd been in this manor the entire time, gathering the energy needed to physically hurt one of his descendants. We all had to be very careful choosing our next move. If I did follow through with our failsafe plan, then we'd be left to deal with Ophelia's ghost after watching us trap her husband's raging spirit. I feared that all her sorrow could easily turn into a tsunami of uncontrolled anger.

One by one, the individual candles that Piper had set out were being extinguished. The drapes covering the windows were moving as if gusts of winds were blowing in from outside, and the blazing fire seemed to become stronger and brighter as Eugene finally materialized by the hearth.

Now might be a good time to get that failsafe plan ready, dear hexed one.

"Eugene," Piper called out softly, catching me off guard that she would put herself all in at the chance of angering a vengeful spirit. With that said, she was buying me time to shift the white oak box with my mind so that it was facing the entity responsible for murder. "We can all feel your rage. Is that why you played a trick on us today in room thirteen?"

I'm sensing that Mr. Eugene didn't appreciate that question.

The wood logs in the blazing fire behind Eugene shifted, which caused glowing embers to spark into the air.

"I'm so sorry, Eugene," Ophelia replied, sadness drenching her words. **"I had no choice but to show them. Please come with me so that we can rest."**

True love...it's unconditional.

Eugene was the spirit who had committed murder.

I wasn't so sure such an evil act didn't change the meaning of love.

It seems not, dear hexed one. Ms. Ophelia wouldn't have remained behind all these years in a state of unrest had her love not been unconditional.

All three Ashtons who were still gripping each other's hands as if they were about to be swept up by a tornado didn't know quite where to focus—on Ophelia hovering near the French doors, Eugene near the hearth, or Piper sitting across from me. We'd never divulged what we'd originally found in room thirteen, which turned out to be a good thing considering it had been nothing but a mirage.

The pieces of the puzzle were beginning to fall into place, and a few more questions might actually solve Florence's murder. In the meantime, I needed to be ready just in case Eugene didn't take Ophelia up on her offer to cross over.

I hadn't realized how much Ms. Ophelia loves her husband, dear hexed one. Locking him inside that box might just create yet another poltergeist underneath the roof of this manor.

"That magic was supposed to ensure the Ashton tradition continued through the generations." Eugene's words were somewhat distorted in an eerie tenor. **"Change the will back to the way it was."**

"Please don't break the circle," Piper requested softly, speaking specifically to Wilbur. The older man had believed it was the Ashtons themselves causing all their problems, even though he knew there to be spirits roaming the estate. "It's important to keep talking to them to find out what happened to Ms. Florence."

Murder, my sweet Piper. The poor woman was murdered in her own home.

"Eugene, look at what you've done," Ophelia said, practically begging her husband to listen to her. She glided across the floor, becoming ever closer to her husband. Faye, Izzy, and Joshua practically shoved the coffee table forward as they attempted to steer clear of

Ophelia. **"You took the life of a family member."**

The one thing you must understand about the supernatural realm was that each day presented something new to us. Even in Pearl's two thousand years, there were still things that occurred for the first time.

Like now. Oh, I'm beginning to need another spot of warm cream.

In between the space that Ophelia had left between her and Eugene, a mirage of some sort appeared as if it were playing on a movie screen. We all stared in disbelief as the night Florence fell to her death was replayed in front of us in full living color.

Eugene was basically begging Florence to change back the will as he followed her down the stairs. Of course, the matriarch couldn't hear him and continued to descend, finally reaching the landing. Eugene's warning came through as clear as day when he all but threatened to take over her body to see to it that things were put back in their rightful place.

We were all wrong, dear hexed one. Mr. Eugene wasn't trying to murder Florence. He wanted to take control of her vessel long enough to ensure that the Ashton family tradition was carried out to his request. It was nothing more than a tragic accident.

"Eugene, you saw to it that our children, our children's children, and so on were taken care of for many generations to come," Ophelia reassured him, though I could still sense Eugene's reluctance to let things be. **"You stayed long enough to see your dreams fulfilled,**

but only our family knows what is right for them on this side of the veil. It's time to rest now, Eugene. Please, come with me."

You realize that it's not that simple for Mr. Eugene to cross through the veil now, right? Regardless that he never intended to kill someone, forgiveness plays a key role in whether a spirit can find peace.

I began to quietly explain to the Ashtons that they had a choice to make. It was clear that Eugene had only meant to protect his legacy, for some reason believing that following tradition was vital. A lot of people back during that time were superstitious, and he'd taken it entirely too seriously.

"He murdered our mother," Joshua whispered fiercely, all the while Ophelia kept trying to coax her husband to join her on the other side. "I can't even believe this is happening! A ghost killed our mother? This is insanity!"

Welcome to our world, Mr. Joshua.

"We can change it back," Faye murmured, keeping her distrustful gaze on the two spirits. She was still frightened, and rightfully so. No one could predict what would happen if his energy became even more vexed than before due to realizing the damage he'd done to his family. "I'll sign the papers, allowing you to run to the estate. All that mattered to me was that my sister understood that our home meant as much to me as it did to her."

Joshua was already shaking his head, apparently having come to terms with his mother's decision. Right now, his anger was focused on Eugene's spirit...and I couldn't blame him one bit.

Forgiveness is not easy, dear hexed one.

There was something in Pearl's words of wisdom that told me there was a deeper meaning to her sentiment, but I was a bit too distracted to ponder on her reply.

"Joshua." Knox surprised everyone by saying the man's name, garnering everyone's attention but the two spirits. Ophelia was openly weeping as the mirage faded away, leaving Eugene near the blazing fire that was only somewhat contained within the hearth. I'd been keeping my attention on the burning logs in case I needed to use my magic to prevent a catastrophe. "It will take you years to accept what has happened to your mother, let alone process what her death has done to your family. Right now, you have two entities that don't belong here. The only way to—"

Knox broke off what he wanted to say versus what was more appropriate, and I gave him credit for his restraint.

I give his mother all the credit. Mrs. Emeric did an amazing job with our hairy colleague, did she not?

"What I'm trying to say is that everyone, including your mother, deserves peace." Knox tilted his head toward the two spirits still communicating with one another by the hearth. "No one believed Ms. Ashton when she tried to tell anyone who would listen that the manor was haunted, and in the end, it cost your mother

her life. She's obviously crossed through the veil, but only the three of you can see to it that the remainder of your family is at peace. It was a tragic and horrifying accident, but don't allow anger to eat away at your soul."

I wonder if it's the lycanthropy that makes him so wise or if his mother just did that good of a job raising him…

"Joshua, they can only remain seen to us for a smidge longer," I announced, already sensing that the energy in the room was waning. "The three of you either offer forgiveness or…"

I'm glad you allowed their imaginations to run away with the latter choice. Mr. Eugene's rage could continue to morph until this manor is no longer inhabitable.

"Ophelia? Eugene?" Izzy called out with a tremor in her voice. She took it upon herself to speak for the family, which was probably for the best. "It's time for the two of you to be at peace. We know that you didn't intend to hurt our mother, and she's waiting for you on the other side."

"Everything I worked for…and I ended up hurting one of my own," Eugene replied in anguish, his fury and guilt easily discernable from the way the blazing fire crackled behind him. **"I gave my life to ensure our family was taken care of after my death. What have I done?"**

"We *are* taken care of, Eugene," Faye explained, tears filling her eyes. "Family meant everything to Florence, and she read those journals every day to become closer to all of you. We will make sure that your legacy is protected. It's time for you to go with Ophelia, the woman who dedicated her life to you. Join her in the afterlife...and find peace."

Izzy was openly crying now, nodding her agreement while she tried unsuccessfully to gain some measure of composure. Truthfully, I wasn't even sure there was a dry eye in the room...and that included me.

And me.

"Patricia and Theodore are waiting for us," Ophelia said softly, holding her ethereal hand out for her husband. **"It's time for us to go, Eugene."**

Part of the energy that contained the rage and guilt began to dissipate slowly, allowing the fire behind the two apparitions to ever so gradually return to its normal size. To show that we trusted these spirits to do as requested, I concentrated on the white oak box until the lid slowly closed.

We no longer needed the failsafe plan.

One can never be too careful, dear hexed one. Speaking of which, what do you suppose ever happened to that voodoo doll?

"My family..."

"Yes, our family," Ophelia agreed with Eugene as the two entities now faced the three Ashtons...including the older couple sitting across from them. **"Gertrude and Wilbur, thank you for taking care of them over the years."**

Now wasn't the time to ask about the voodoo doll or where Eugene had come into such an item. I didn't want to be the reason he stayed behind. He and his wife had been trapped here for far too long as it was.

True, but I've always had a hard time with pesky loose ends. Another quick peek throughout the manor couldn't hurt, could it?

"I'm so sorry for the pain I've caused." Eugene's remorse was evident. The very act of misfortune he'd committed in this very mansion had been his worst fear—hurting his family. **"I never intended…"**

"We know," Izzy replied with a small hiccup as she finally regained some of that composure she'd been seeking.

"Rest in peace," Faye and Joshua both said in unison, their heartfelt farewell seemingly doing the trick.

We all watched in amazement as Ophelia and Eugene gradually faded away, crossing through the veil to join their children. The rhythmic ticking of the grandfather clock seemed to be louder than before, filling the silent void that remained behind with their departure.

Beautiful. Just beautiful.

Pearl's reply to Ophelia and Eugene crossing over into the afterlife told me that I was definitely a bit jaded.

Really? I wouldn't have guessed.

I'm just saying that I'm not so sure I could have been as forgiving as the Ashtons. It took a special person to be able to reach that level of peace, and quite honestly…I was envious.

I'm sure there's a self-help app we could find on your phone to help you with that itsy-bitsy problem.

"Normally at the close of a séance, I would thank the spirits for joining us," I began, ignoring Pearl. Besides, I had no doubt that curiosity would get the best of her, and she would roam the manor and the grounds of the estate to ensure that the voodoo doll was not somewhere on the property. "Seeing as they've already crossed over, I'll just leave it at this—rest in peace, Ophelia and Eugene."

I loosened my grip on Orwin and Joshua's hands, prompting them to do the same with the others. Izzy and Faye held each other, with Joshua rubbing his sister's shoulder in empathy. After all, it wasn't every day that the families of those murdered got this type of closure.

Piper and Orwin concentrated on Gertrude and Wilbur, who were in somewhat of a state of shock after witnessing such a phenomenon. The older couple seemed out of breath, but I had a feeling they wouldn't be leaving at first light. Gertrude even reached across the coffee table, offering her hand to Faye. The two women clasped each other's fingers in comfort, seeking solace in each other's shared experience.

Another case had ended, offering Knox and I a chance to find a cure to these hexes that had taken over our lives. If Ammeline Letty Romilda stood in front of us and asked for forgiveness, I wasn't so sure I'd be able to give mine.

What did that say about me and who I am?

Miss Lilura, you do everything in your power to ensure that those victims in your visions do not meet the fate you see for them. I daresay that says a lot about your true character. No one can reach perfection, dear hexed one…not even you.

Chapter Fifteen

MORNING HAD DAWNED bright and early, but I slept through the sunrise. I hadn't even wanted to crawl out of bed at noon. That exhaustion I'd been fighting had won, and I'd all but crawled up to my room and fallen into bed shortly after bringing the séance to a close.

Piper wasn't even in the room when I opened my eyes, which led me to believe she was already downstairs with the others.

"Pearl?"

No answer.

It was a toss-up as to whether the know-it-all familiar was searching the manor for the elusive voodoo doll or she was in the kitchen enjoying a spot of warm cream before we hit the road back to the campsite and our expensive mobile Batcave.

I'd wanted to follow up with our conversation last night about perfection, but I guess that discussion would have to wait until later.

I wasn't seeking perfection.

At least, I didn't believe I was pursuing such an unattainable goal.

I'd put it this way—I was searching for a way to get my life back.

Today was another day to reach that objective, so I tossed the comforter to the side to get ready for our next case. Of course, that case was regarding a medium and my hex. Either way, it was rare that I got this amount of privacy in the morning. I was going to enjoy every minute of the peace and quiet.

An hour later, I was carrying my bag down the long and winding staircase. Not a blip of energy could be sensed near the landing. It was good to know that this manor was now cleansed and could return to its normal operation after so many years.

"…if we advertise on the travel sites."

"…bring in more revenue for the upkeep of the grounds."

"I love that idea. What do you think about…"

I smiled upon hearing the Ashtons having a family meeting in the great room. No animosity could be heard, and there was no doubt that the Ashton Manor would remain open to the public. Their history should be shared, and those remaining relatives would see to it that Eugene's legacy continued on.

I didn't even tell you a knock-knock joke.

"Good morning, Pearl," I replied quietly, still grinning at another successful case. "Did you ever find your voodoo doll?"

Unfortunately, no. Let's just hope that such an object remains buried. Like you, I'd hate to see the truce this family has accomplished to all be for naught.

It was good that I hadn't responded to Pearl's concern immediately, for Gertrude was standing behind the high-top desk in the small alcove in the foyer. It was one thing for her, Wilbur, and the Ashtons to think we were some type of paranormal investigation team...it was entirely another to explain that we were witches.

And a werewolf. I'd say that Mr. Emeric came through for us extremely well last night, wouldn't you?

"Good morning, Ms. Lilura," Gertrude greeted, having just finished talking with Piper. The two women were grinning as if they were in on a secret. "You missed breakfast, but I can whip you up something for lunch. It won't take me—"

"Thank you, Gertrude, but I'll just grab something on the road." I crossed the marble tiles, setting my overnight bag on the cold floor. "How is everyone this morning?"

"Still in shock," Gertrude answered honestly. She gestured toward the great room. "But Wilbur and I are very grateful for the outcome. This is our home, too, and we were devastated to have made the decision to leave. That's changed now, thanks to all of you."

"I'm glad things worked out for you." I didn't hesitate to reach out and allow the older woman to hold my hand. "If you ever have any...problems, please call us."

You never cease to amaze me, dear hexed one. I don't believe I've ever heard you make such an offer before. Progress.

I resisted the urge to roll my eyes. There had been a small coffee machine that made individual cups in our suite, but I hadn't consumed nearly enough caffeine to banter with Pearl.

My sweet Piper made sure I had my breakfast this morning, along with a spot of warm cream. Delicious. Just delicious.

"Orwin, Knox, and I have already said our good-byes," Piper said, holding the strap of her cross-body purse. She must have stored her bag in the Jeep while I'd been sleeping. "They're outside, ready when you are."

Now might be a good time to let you know that the alien hunter plans on taking a quick detour. It's a good thing I'm riding back with you and my sweet Piper. I'm not so sure I can stand to hear another thought about a UFO somewhere at the bottom of Lake Superior.

"Gertrude, thank you for everything."

"No, dear. Thank you," Gertrude reiterated with a small smile, squeezing my fingers a little tighter in gratitude. "Now, you go on in and say goodbye to the Ashtons. They're expecting you."

Piper soundlessly stepped away and made her way out the front door, while I reluctantly walked over to the French doors. I would have preferred to slip out quietly, but I understood their need for closure. Thankfully, our goodbyes were short and sweet, with the promise if we ever needed anything in return…all we had to do was call.

Another first. You realize that garnering favors isn't such a bad thing, Ms. Lilura. One never knows what resources we'll need in the future.

With a final wave to Gertrude and Wilbur, who'd joined her at the counter, I was finally able to draw a breath of the refreshing air outside. Fall had definitely arrived, if the chilly temperature was anything to go by.

"Let me get your bag for you." I wasn't sure if Knox had been walking the grounds and happened to be near the door when I exited the manor or if he'd been waiting for me. "Did you get enough sleep?"

How kind of him to ask. Did I mention that I'd love to meet his mother? She did an exceptional job raising such a gentleman.

"Yes, I did," I replied, relinquishing my hold of the handle. I was glad I'd put on my black leather jacket. The gusts of wind coming across the grounds were rather sharp. "I appreciate you guys waiting for me. I crashed hard after last night."

"It's understandable." Knox shortened his stride to mine, letting me know that he had something he wanted to say without the others listening in. "Listen, I appreciate you taking my reservations about this case seriously."

I could sense that Pearl had given us privacy, which wasn't surprising given her propensity for etiquette.

"Knox, there's a lot about the supernatural that you haven't learned." I slipped my hands in the pockets of my jacket to keep them warm. The sun was resting behind some clouds, preventing its warmth from touching my skin. "There are things that even I haven't encountered, but that's due to my wanting to live a normal life. Had I stayed with the coven, I might have been better prepared to deal with Ammeline."

"I don't believe anyone could be prepared enough to meet up with something so vile," Knox muttered, stopping in the middle of the cobblestone drive. We were around twenty feet from the others. He was definitely learning the limitations of our abilities. "I didn't mean to overstep last night."

"What?" I asked, his apology catching me off guard. "Knox, you didn't overstep at all. It was a group effort, and I'm honestly not sure what the Ashtons would have done had you not given them that advice."

"You don't believe in forgiveness?"

Knox's question practically stole my breath away. It was one thing to have this intimate conversation with Pearl, where I didn't necessarily have to say the words aloud. Telling the truth would definitely have Knox seeing me in a different light, but his inference that he could forgive easily had changed mine of his.

"And you can?" I asked, tossing the question back his way.

From the lift at the corner of his mouth, he recognized the defensive tactic.

"Serving in the military taught me a lot, but to an-

swer your question…I'm not sure. Forgiving a person—
or soul, in this case—is different. People are fallible.
Everyone makes mistakes. Ammeline? I'm not so sure she
has a soul, and that changes everything for me."

"We'll cross that bridge when we come to it."

"That we will," Knox murmured in agreement, seeming to want to say more but turning back toward the
others. "Just out of curiosity, how serious is Orwin about
this crazy UFO business?"

"I guess you'll find out soon enough," I replied with
a light laugh, advancing forward toward Piper, Pearl, and
Orwin. The familiar had materialized inside the open
driver's side door and was currently sitting on the middle
console of the Jeep. "We'll meet the two of you back at
camp."

*A laugh, dear hexed one? Hmmm. I think we might
have just found out what lightens the burden on your
shoulders.*

"Our detour shouldn't take but an hour." Orwin
pushed up his glasses as he quickly made his way around
Knox's Land Rover. His nose was practically glued to the
screen of his cell phone, no doubt reading up on the
Lake Superior claim. "Knox, are you ready?"

Knox had taken the time to store my bag in the back
of the Jeep. He'd already closed the back hatch and was
palming the keys to his vehicle. He sighed in resignation,
probably not able to ascertain how he'd come to be the
chauffeur of our resident conspiracy theorist.

He could join the club, because I'd never thought we'd be something akin to supernatural ghostbusters, either. Right now, we needed to get as much information from our own ancestors about Ammeline's power as we could. That meant using a medium who could harness enough energy to draw forth the leaders of the covens from the past. That wasn't an easy feat, by any means.

"We'll reach out to Cassandra Saruman tomorrow," I said, ignoring Pearl's attempt at making more out of my relationship with Knox than friendship. We were bonded by our curses, nothing else. "It's time to meet this medium in person."

You couldn't allow one minute of lightheartedness, Miss Lilura? You realize what I must do, right?

"Please don't," I muttered, settling inside the driver's seat of the Jeep and plugging the nearest coffee place into the GPS. "Not enough caffeine."

"Just go with it," Piper suggested, knowing her familiar better than anyone. "Pearl might have complained about the app on my phone this entire case, but she certainly wasn't complaining when I pulled up a site that contained a bunch of new knock-knock jokes."

The dangers of technology are no laughing matter, my sweet Piper. But one must learn to adapt, which is what I shall try to do in the future.

"Traitor," I quipped back to Piper, wondering just how many knock-knock jokes a familiar could learn in the span of a few minutes.

Knock-knock.

"It's best to get this over with," Piper advised with a big smile.

I had a sneaking suspicion she enjoyed watching Pearl irritate me, so I finally caved and asked the question.

"Who's there?" I inquired reluctantly, shifting the gear into reverse.

Abbott.

"Abbott who?"

Abbott time we solved this mystery, dear hexed one.

I didn't want to smile. I really didn't, but Piper's laugh was infectious. Having these lighthearted moments wasn't so bad, especially when we didn't know what awaited us down the road.

Maybe, just maybe, the cure to my hex was at the end of this road trip.

~ THE END ~

Thank you so much for joining Lou and the gang as they continue to solve the murder mysteries that she sees in her visions! The next tale involves bats, fangs, and vampires in *The Curse that Bites*…this is one you won't want to miss!

kennedylayne.com/the-curse-that-bites.html

A cloud of bats is whipping up an exciting whodunit in the latest installment in the Hex on Me Mysteries by USA Today Bestselling Author Kennedy Layne…

Lou and the gang become stranded when their brand-new RV breaks down in the middle of Podunk, USA. They soon realize that their arrival in this tiny town might not be by happenstance. Their situation becomes exceptionally dire when Lou has another premonition of murder…this time, the victim is one of their very own group!

A garlic necklace might be an appropriate accessory to bring along for this evening's entertainment, as this tale promises to be as wickedly sharp as the tip on the end of a wooden stake!

Books by Kennedy Layne

Hex on Me Mysteries
If the Curse Fits
Cursing up the Wrong Tree
The Squeaky Ghost Gets the Curse
The Curse that Bites

Paramour Bay Mysteries
Magical Blend
Bewitching Blend
Enchanting Blend
Haunting Blend
Charming Blend
Spellbinding Blend
Cryptic Blend
Broomstick Blend

Office Roulette Series
Means (Office Roulette, Book One)
Motive (Office Roulette, Book Two)
Opportunity (Office Roulette, Book Three)

Keys to Love Series
Unlocking Fear (Keys to Love, Book One)
Unlocking Secrets (Keys to Love, Book Two)
Unlocking Lies (Keys to Love, Book Three)
Unlocking Shadows (Keys to Love, Book Four)
Unlocking Darkness (Keys to Love, Book Five)

Surviving Ashes Series
Essential Beginnings (Surviving Ashes, Book One)

Hidden Ashes (Surviving Ashes, Book Two)
Buried Flames (Surviving Ashes, Book Three)
Endless Flames (Surviving Ashes, Book Four)
Rising Flames (Surviving Ashes, Book Five)

CSA CASE FILES SERIES
Captured Innocence (CSA Case Files 1)
Sinful Resurrection (CSA Case Files 2)
Renewed Faith (CSA Case Files 3)
Campaign of Desire (CSA Case Files 4)
Internal Temptation (CSA Case Files 5)
Radiant Surrender (CSA Case Files 6)
Redeem My Heart (CSA Case Files 7)
A Mission of Love (CSA Case Files 8)

RED STARR SERIES
Starr's Awakening(Red Starr, Book One)
Hearths of Fire (Red Starr, Book Two)
Targets Entangled (Red Starr, Book Three)
Igniting Passion (Red Starr, Book Four)
Untold Devotion (Red Starr, Book Five)
Fulfilling Promises (Red Starr, Book Six)
Fated Identity (Red Starr, Book Seven)
Red's Salvation (Red Starr, Book Eight)

THE SAFEGUARD SERIES
Brutal Obsession (The Safeguard Series, Book One)
Faithful Addiction (The Safeguard Series, Book Two)
Distant Illusions (The Safeguard Series, Book Three)
Casual Impressions (The Safeguard Series, Book Four)
Honest Intentions (The Safeguard Series, Book Five)
Deadly Premonitions (The Safeguard Series, Book Six)

ABOUT THE AUTHOR

First and foremost, I love life. I love that I'm a wife, mother, daughter, sister... and a writer.

I am one of the lucky women in this world who gets to do what makes them happy. As long as I have a cup of coffee (maybe two or three) and my laptop, the stories evolve themselves and I try to do them justice. I draw my inspiration from a retired Marine Master Sergeant that swept me off of my feet and has drawn me into a world that fulfills all of my deepest and darkest desires. Erotic romance, military men, intrigue, with a little bit of kinky chili pepper (his recipe), fill my head and there is nothing more satisfying than making the hero and heroine fulfill their destinies.

Thank you for having joined me on their journeys...

Email: kennedylayneauthor@gmail.com

Facebook: facebook.com/kennedy.layne.94

Twitter: twitter.com/KennedyL_Author

Website: www.kennedylayne.com

Newsletter:
www.kennedylayne.com/aboutnewsletter.html